Throw His Heart Over

an Aubrey & Lindsey novel

by Sebastian Nothwell

DEDICATION

To Janet, Lou, and Olivia, for making this book possible.

CONTENTS

CHAPTER ONE

London, England
July 1892

"A toast," Sir Lindsey Althorp declared, raising his champagne flute and standing from his seat at the head of the dinner table. The flickering candlelight of the crystal chandelier sparkled down through the white-gold bubbles. "To a beautiful bride-to-be and her attending angels. The City of Light will shine all the brighter for your presence in it."

His guests agreed heartily and with much cheer. Lindsey himself clinked glasses to his right with the subject of his toast—one Miss Emmeline Rook, soon to become Lady Emmeline Althorp, when he married her June next. She bit her lip as she smiled, her blush bringing the faintest hint of pink to her otherwise colourless features. The shimmering silk of her bright chartreuse gown proved colour enough, in Lindsey's opinion.

To his left, the rim of his glass struck that of one Mr Aubrey Warren and rang with such a true, clear note as if to underscore his own feelings for the man. To Lindsey's eyes, Aubrey always looked quite handsome—the fine-boned delicacy of his features offsetting the dashing burn scar running from his chin to his ear—but Lindsey thought he looked particularly becoming tonight, in sleek black-and-white evening attire tailored so close to his slender frame. The smile Aubrey gave as they toasted made him handsomer still, bringing joyful warmth to his deep brown eyes and a beguiling curve to his

1

Cupid's bow lips.

"Hear, hear," came a voice from further down the table, drawing Lindsey's attention away from his beloved.

The speaker was one Lord Cyril Graves, third son of an inconsequential Marquess and Lindsey's old school friend. He sat on Emmeline's other side and across the table from Miss Rowena Althorp, Lindsey's own sister, and the true hostess, no matter what her seating arrangement might imply. These smaller, more informal dinners between the siblings' closest friends tended to turn etiquette on its head. If they continued down this road, they'd end up almost Bohemian.

A more Bohemian dinner would well suit his other gentleman guest, Mr John Halloway—an artist by trade, and Graves's particular companion by choice. He sat next to Rowena and across from Lady Charity Pelham, the dignified young widow who would *chaperon* Rowena and Emmeline on their impending sojourn. The ladies were to set sail upon the morrow for Calais and journey to Paris, where they would spend the next month or two acquiring a new wardrobe for Emmeline from the House of Worth, including her wedding gown, and likely a few dresses for Rowena as well.

The toast ended, Lindsey resumed his seat and turned his attention to the conversation closer at hand.

"I do wish you could come, Aubrey," Emmeline was saying to Lindsey's beloved. "Eiffel's tower is reason enough!"

Aubrey demurred with a sidelong glance at Rowena. "I don't think I'd be much help picking out dresses."

"Really, Emmeline," Rowena drawled. "I wish you were even half as interested in choosing your wedding gown. To hear you tell it, one would think we were going to Paris purely for the pleasure of riding a packet steamer."

"Oh, but I trust your taste implicitly!" Emmeline assured her, undaunted.

"Just so long as you don't try to walk down the aisle in chartreuse," Rowena murmured into her wineglass.

Emmeline went on to describe in exhaustive detail the technical specifications of the packet steamer the ladies would take across the Channel. Aubrey, her equal in engineering, listened attentively. Lindsey followed along as best he could, until the end of the dessert, at which point Emmeline and the other ladies withdrew, leaving the gentlemen to liquor and conversation unrestrained by sensitivity to feminine ears. Not that the ladies could possibly find anything to object to in the resulting conversation of these particular gentlemen.

"Really," Graves said as the door closed upon the ladies' skirts, "I don't think Doyle's last effort quite up to the standard set by his previous works."

"Thought you considered Doyle beneath your touch," Halloway observed dryly.

Graves, evidently well-accustomed to such barbs from his artist, scoffed. "One can hardly escape him! It's all anyone will talk of in the clubs. Besides, my position obliges me to read a wide variety, for better comparison."

Lindsey well knew Graves referred not to his position as a member of the aristocracy, but his position as a literary critic for certain fashionable publications. "You have compared Doyle to himself, then, and found him lacking—in your opinion."

"I have," Graves conceded. "*The Adventure of the Copper Beeches* is nothing when contrasted against *A Study in Scarlet*."

"You must wonder why Dr Watson took the trouble to record it," Lindsey replied, smiling.

"I liked it," said Aubrey.

A surprised silence descended upon the table—tinged with delight on Lindsey's part and disbelief on Graves's. Halloway, meanwhile, swirled his port in his glass and sat back to watch with the air of one anticipating a most amusing show.

"I had rather thought," Graves began, then stopped himself with a glance at Lindsey.

Whatever barb Graves had chosen to suppress, Lindsey felt grateful for his efforts. His Aubrey had suffered under Graves's slings and arrows before, and Lindsey would not stand to see him suffer so again.

Tonight, however, Aubrey appeared to anticipate the attack. Raising his pointed chin, he replied in a perfectly even voice, "You had rather thought I might prefer *The Adventure of the Engineer's Thumb*."

Graves glanced at Lindsey again before replying, in more muted tones, "Indeed."

Aubrey took the jab at his profession much more coolly than Lindsey would have done on his behalf. "You're correct. I'm very fond of that one. Though I cannot argue for its literary merit, on account of my own bias. I suppose you prefer *The Adventure of the Noble Bachelor?*"

Halloway's bark of laughter quite overpowered whatever initial reply Graves might have made. Lindsey couldn't help joining in; a glance at Aubrey found him likewise affected, though in a more reserved manner, his humour present only in his dark eyes and the smallest tug at the corners of his bow-shaped lips.

In waiting for silence, Graves had time to craft a more measured response. When the noise died down, he said, "*The Noble Bachelor* is well enough for the masses. I maintain, however, that nothing yet matches the intrigue of *A Study in Scarlet.* And indeed, nothing Doyle has produced rivals Wilde."

"Actually," Halloway interrupted, having recovered from his bout of mirth, "he's fond of *The Blue Carbuncle.*"

"Really?" said Lindsey, turning upon his friend. "I'd have thought that too Dickensian for your taste."

Graves, attempting to hide his red face behind his wineglass, muttered, "You're all bastards."

Aubrey chuckled—then surprised Lindsey again by asking Graves, "What do you consider Wilde's best work?"

Graves looked at him warily, then, upon judging his inquiry to be sincere, began speaking upon *The Picture of Dorian Gray*, and quickly warmed to his subject—the sheer illicit pleasure of such decadent prose proving Wilde's mastery over the English language, etc. His discourse carried the gentlemen on to the hour when etiquette deemed it prudent to rejoin the ladies in the drawing room.

"Rowena," Lindsey asked the moment he crossed the drawing room threshold. "Your favourite Holmes adventure—which is it?"

Rowena, seated betwixt Emmeline and Lady Pelham in a circle of matching armchairs, answered without hesitation. "*A Scandal in Bohemia.*"

Lindsey supposed he ought to have guessed as much. Graves, for his part, declared he'd already known it. Aubrey, meanwhile, had no sooner entered the drawing room than Emmeline leapt up to seize his elbow and resume their engineering discussion as if it'd never been interrupted.

Later that evening, the guests all drifted to their respective chambers for the night, and Lindsey caught up to Aubrey at last in the hallway just outside the master bedroom.

"You know," Lindsey said as he laid his hand upon the small of Aubrey's back, "I'm rather fond of *The Engineer's Thumb* myself. And other parts besides."

Aubrey chuckled. "I'm just glad Graves wanted to talk about something I've actually read, for once."

Lindsey, his brow furrowed, opened his mouth to enquire further.

"Lindsey," came his sister's voice from behind him.

Interrupted, Lindsey spun to find Rowena standing at the other end of the hall.

With a speaking glance, Aubrey pressed Lindsey's hand and slipped away into the master bedroom, leaving Lindsey alone in the hall with his sister.

Rowena, having approached in the meantime, addressed him just as the bedroom door clicked shut. "Before we depart, there's something I must charge you with in my absence."

"Name it," declared Lindsey, still bewildered.

"Select a girl or two from the country house for your Manchester staff."

Lindsey blinked at her. "Pardon?"

"You're about to add a bride to your household," Rowena explained. "Charles might do well enough caring for a pair of gentlemen, but a lady has further requirements."

"I rather thought that end of the business would be left up to Emmeline."

Rowena paused. Lindsey recognised her expression well: the parted lips, stopped tongue, and sidelong glance she wore when she had a ready and honest answer, but required careful wording to avoid giving offence. "I believe Emmeline's talents are better suited to the refitting of the house for electrical power. At least, she seems determined to expend all her energy upon it, and I doubt she will have much left over for the general keeping of your house."

Lindsey understood her as perfectly as if she'd said outright that Emmeline couldn't supervise domestic staff if her very life depended upon it.

"Besides," Rowena continued, "the wedding isn't until next June. It seems woefully unfair to expect Charles to continue on by himself for almost a year. He has enough to do as your valet, and since you established your residence in Manchester, he's become something of a girl-of-all-work as well."

Charles did have rather a lot to occupy him, Lindsey supposed. Though, upon reflection, many of Charles's former duties as Lindsey's valet—brushing suits, polishing boots, the general tidying-up of the master bedroom—had been taken on by Aubrey, mostly out of Aubrey's stubborn streak of independence and quiet refusal to allow anyone but himself to see to his wardrobe. As he'd said when Lindsey had suggested Charles might see to the shoe-horns, he'd managed well enough on his own for the last four-and-twenty years and didn't see any reason to stop now.

Rowena, heedless of Lindsey's interior monologue, added, "To say nothing of how much more smoothly the transition from bachelor life to wedded bliss shall prove if the staff are already in place and settled into their routine."

Lindsey had to concede her reasoning appeared sound, though he hardly considered himself a true bachelor now that he'd found his Aubrey. "Would you recommend anyone in particular?"

"Anyone from the country house would suit," she replied. "They're all used to our... peculiarities. And I'm sure many of the maids would leap at the chance to move to a city. It would give them a far better chance of finding husbands." In response to Lindsey's confused expression, she added, "It isn't as though any of the footmen would do them the honours."

Lindsey, well aware of his sister's curious hiring practises—to whit, taking on only confirmed bachelors in her efforts to waylay any attempt at blackmail by the staff—hadn't before considered its effects on the marriage prospects of the female servants.

"Emmeline will, of course, bring over Bessie as her lady's maid," Rowena went on blithely, regardless of his reply or lack thereof.

It took Lindsey a moment to recognise the name of his *fiancée*'s former girl-of-all-work.

"However," said Rowena in response to no one but herself. "I would recommend you recruit at least one other housemaid—ideally two—and take on one of the kitchen-maids as your new cook."

"As you wish," replied Lindsey.

She gave him a warm smile, kissed his cheek, and bid him goodnight.

Lindsey entered his bedroom at last, but whatever questions he had for Aubrey stilled upon his tongue. Aubrey's suit was already hung up, laid out, and folded away, with Aubrey himself already abed. His sharp cheek lay against the soft pillow, the heavy lids of his soulful eyes had shut, and his porcelain brow unfurrowed by any waking concerns.

Lindsey, unwilling to rouse his sleeping angel, slipped silently into bed beside him, and as he turned towards him, had the satisfaction of semi-conscious arms wrapping themselves 'round his shoulders, and so allowed Aubrey to pull him down into sleep.

~

Over the course of the past few months, breakfast had become Aubrey's favourite meal of the day. Not just for its offerings—which, as he regarded the sideboard laden with steaming hot muffins, scones, and sausage, crisp bacon and toast, and an embarrassment of eggs, he had to admit proved considerable in quality and quantity alike—but for its solitude. In the London townhouse, breakfast was the only meal not presided over by at least one servant. As such, it was the only meal he had in town where he didn't feel as though his every move were scrutinised for defect.

As an early riser, he'd grown accustomed to beginning the meal alone. Today, however, he found Halloway already at the table, making neat work of sausage and eggs.

"Graves is having a lie-in," Halloway offered by way of greeting.

Aubrey withheld a wistful smile as he recalled how peaceful Lindsey had appeared when he'd left him scant minutes ago. "And the ladies?"

"Gone. Hours ago. Probably on-board the packet by now."

Aubrey took in this intelligence as he filled a plate with selective offerings. When he turned back to the table, he found Halloway had pulled out a chair beside him.

"I haven't forgotten your promise," said Halloway as Aubrey sat down.

It took Aubrey a moment to remember his own pledge. "To model for you, you mean."

"Yes. If you're still willing."

"I am."

"Splendid. When?"

Aubrey hesitated. When he'd initially agreed to model for

Halloway, he'd done so impulsively, and only after the Rook Mill boiler explosion had burned away half of the features that had inspired Halloway to paint him in the first place. They hadn't agreed on a date and had only barely agreed on a subject.

"Icarus, wasn't it?" Aubrey offered, as if his hazy memory surrounding this detail prevented him from deciding when he would model. He still didn't know who or what Icarus was—he'd meant to ask Lindsey about it at the time, but so much had happened since that he'd quite forgotten.

"Icarus, indeed," Halloway confirmed, still giving no hint as to the definition of an Icarus. "Whenever it's convenient for you."

Aubrey reviewed his mental calendar. "The electrical conversion of the mill will have to wait until Emmeline returns from Paris, so there's not terrible much for me to do while she's gone. I suppose I could be free as early as this week. Unless Lindsey has something planned."

"What are we planning?" asked Lindsey, appearing just then upon the threshold, his entrance warming the room like a beam of sunshine.

"Painting Warren as Icarus," Halloway repeated. "It'll take some doing to transform my rooms into the rocky seashore, but we'll manage somehow."

Aubrey recalled his old lodging house, where Halloway still had his studio. A cramped little flat in a back-street of Manchester, dim thanks to the perpetual smog, and draughty thanks to Halloway keeping the windows open all hours to let out the paint fumes. Aubrey didn't look forward to returning. Still, he had made a promise, and he intended to keep it.

Lindsey, meanwhile, appeared thoughtful as he filled his plate at the sideboard and approached the table. "Would it be more convenient for you to paint somewhere else?"

"Did you have someplace in mind?" asked Halloway, looking as curious as Aubrey felt.

"The Wiltshire house is rather commodious," Lindsey replied, sitting down on Aubrey's other side. "Plenty of light, quiet seclusion, great big windows for ventilation—more than enough room for you to paint in, if you'd prefer. We could all stay there for a holiday whilst we wait for Rowena *et al* to return from Paris."

A wave of relief washed over Aubrey. He pressed Lindsey's hand under the table, and felt a firm clasp in return.

Halloway appeared intrigued. "If you're offering, then I'd be delighted to accept."

"Accept what?" Graves grumbled, shoving his hair out of his eyes as he shuffled through the doorway.

"An invitation to a country holiday in Wiltshire," Lindsey summarised for him, his own ebullient demeanour unchanged by his friend's sour entrance. "Halloway's going to paint Aubrey. You're welcome to join us."

"In the middle of the season?" Graves asked as if he couldn't quite believe his ears. "I'm afraid I'll have to decline. I've far too many engagements yet in town. Can't get away to the country until the first hunt, at the earliest."

All the better from Aubrey's perspective. Though he and Graves maintained a politeness between them, for Lindsey's sake, it wasn't an easy one. Graves hadn't thought much of workhouse brats before Aubrey came along, and Aubrey got the impression he didn't think much better of them now, despite Lindsey's partiality.

Halloway cast an indulgent look at Graves. "In that case, I'm afraid you'll have to do without me until then. I simply cannot pass up such an opportunity."

Graves sniffed, which Halloway seemed to understand as a concession, as he patted Graves's hand in sympathy.

"The ballroom is probably best suited to your needs," Lindsey went on, peering into the middle distance as if he saw his country house before him in his mind. He added in an apologetic tone, "Not that I know much about art."

"All I need is space and light," Halloway reassured him. "And Warren's assistance. I'll provide the rest."

"Do you have a composition in mind?" asked Lindsey. Aubrey, too, felt no small measure of curiosity.

"Several," Halloway replied. "I believe my sketch-book is in the guest room..."

Lindsey dispatched Charles to retrieve the sketch-book. When Halloway had it in his hands, he wasted no time in flipping it open to a blank page and demonstrating his idea.

"We'll have you stretched out like this," Halloway said to Aubrey, his pencil dashing across the page to bring his vision to life. "And the wings will fold over here, like so..."

Aubrey watched, amazed, as before his very eyes emerged, from nothing, the image of a nude man, reclining on his side, with one arm above his head and another lying limp before him, and his hips canted towards the viewer, with anything objectionable covered by a broken wing strapped to his shoulder—the other wing spread beneath him.

"Think you can do it?" Halloway asked.

"Do I have to wear the wings?" Aubrey replied.

Halloway chuckled. "I might need to tie a few belts to your arms, but no—the wings will remain mere fantasy."

Aubrey, who hadn't realised the painting would involve wings at all until Halloway had begun sketching, tried to look as though he'd known all along that, of course, there would be wings. "Seems doable to me."

Lindsey, meanwhile, had come around to peer over their shoulders at the sketch. "By Jove, that's grand!"

Aubrey glanced towards him only to have his own attention arrested by the evident joy writ across Lindsey's handsome features. Lindsey's enthusiasm proved infectious as ever, and Aubrey found himself smiling down at the sketch in turn.

~

Aubrey hadn't returned to the Wiltshire house since the boiler explosion at Rook Mill. He and Lindsey had spent the bulk of their time in Chorlton-cum-Hardy, just outside of Manchester. They preferred it for proximity to the mill whilst Aubrey oversaw its reconstruction and future conversion to electrical power, as well as for the excitement of life in the thrumming mechanical heart of England. Every week or so they stayed overnight at the London house for one of Rowena's dinner parties or a more casual gathering at Lord Graves's rooms in Pont Street.

But Aubrey had seen nothing of the country since his accident. Nor had the country seen anything of him.

They set out from the London townhouse after breakfast— Halloway returning to Manchester for his painting supplies, and Graves retreating to his own rooms in Pont Street. Lindsey and Aubrey went straight to the train station and arrived in Wiltshire in the evening, just in time for dinner—a very late one, by the standards of country hours. The family carriage, painted gleaming black with the Althorp crest rendered in silver upon its door, awaited them at the train station. If the coachman and groom who attended the horses had any forewarning of what'd become of Aubrey's face, it evidently hadn't been enough. Even by the glow of gaslight, Aubrey saw their eyes widen and their cheeks drain of colour—though, of course, neither one said anything aloud about it. And both, to their credit, recovered quick enough to perform their duties as expected.

When last Aubrey had passed between the pair of enormous marble lions flanking the front steps into the Wiltshire house, he'd had a far more symmetrical face. Now, as he and Lindsey disembarked from the carriage, Aubrey wore the scaly scars from his steam burns over his right cheek, stretching from chin to ear.

The grooms, already inured to the sight of Aubrey's face, showed no further discomfort as they held the carriage door open. Likewise, when the enormous pair of oaken doors to the house swung inward to reveal the butler, Mr Hudson, he too maintained his stone-faced expression as he bowed them in.

But as Aubrey followed Lindsey further into the house, he couldn't help noticing it seemed busier than it had before. Every corner turned, every threshold crossed, every corridor passed down contained at least one footman or maid scurrying out of sight. Aubrey told himself he and Lindsey had caught the staff in the midst of readying the house for their unexpected arrival. This comforting lie didn't survive the sight of one maid gawking in horror as he passed an open doorway to the room she dusted.

Lindsey appeared to notice nothing of the sort, and Aubrey didn't want to bring the mood down by mentioning it while they changed clothes and went down to dinner.

In the dining room, a splendid meal was laid out on the sideboard *a la Française*, though Aubrey knew Lindsey probably considered it simple fare. Charles, Lindsey's omnipresent valet, stood ready by the sideboard. Since Charles went wherever Lindsey led, Aubrey had grown used to his presence in the Chorlton-cum-Hardy house. But here in Wiltshire, a footman stood by the sideboard as well, and Aubrey thought he caught him staring at his half-melted face before Charles dismissed him and, at a nod from Lindsey, followed him out.

Lindsey remained oblivious as he carved the roast and served it to Aubrey. He kept up a constant lighthearted chatter, talking of what fun Rowena must be having in Paris with the freedom to choose all Emmeline's *trousseau*, and what sport might be had in the countryside whilst Aubrey sat for Halloway's painting. Aubrey kept up with him well enough, though not without a twinge of guilt for his own inattention. He felt all too preoccupied with the staff's reaction to his new face.

"...and of course, I'll need your opinion in the matter," Lindsey concluded.

Aubrey, caught out at last, felt a shameful blush flare in his cheeks. "Forgive me, what matter?"

Lindsey appeared somewhat surprised but by no means offended by the question. "The matter of selecting staff to join our household in Manchester."

Aubrey stared at him. He considered the lack of servants a major point of advantage to living in the house at Chorlton-cum-Hardy. Though it hardly seemed prudent to say as much now. Particularly with listening ears around every corner.

"At the very least," Lindsey continued, as if sensing Aubrey needed more information to work with, "we require a cook and a housemaid."

"I like Charles's cooking," said Aubrey. The simple fare Charles threw together every day for the two supposed bachelors settled in Aubrey's stomach far easier than the fancier entrees presented at Rowena's feasts or Graves's *soirées*.

"As do I," said Lindsey, interrupting Aubrey's musing on whether or not Lindsey missed the taste of finer food. "But he does have rather a lot to do as the only staff in the house and well deserves the assistance other servants might provide."

Aubrey couldn't deny the point. When he'd first shacked up with Lindsey, he'd spent rather too much time wondering when in the blazes Charles found a minute to sleep. The man did everything—at least, everything outside of the master bedroom, where Aubrey had gradually taken over the business of keeping things in order.

"To that end," Lindsey continued, "Rowena thought we might recruit some of the maids here to join us in Chorlton-cum-Hardy. And so I'm asking your opinion on which maids will come along to Manchester."

Aubrey's sole experience with household staff thus far had consisted of brief stays in Lindsey's larger establishments—the

Wiltshire house, in which tonight marked only his third visit, and the London townhouse, which he saw with greater frequency and yet which remained more Rowena's household than her brother's—and his former landlady at the boarding house in Manchester, who insisted she was not a housekeeper at every opportunity, despite fulfilling all the duties of the position. And Charles, of course. But Charles aside, Aubrey found he hadn't yet grown accustomed to life with servants. Even the word—servants—felt odd rattling around his brain; it seemed to bespeak an earlier age, without the benefit of electricity or even gaslight. Downright feudal. It didn't sit well with him.

Yet explaining as much to Lindsey felt impossible.

So instead of explaining, Aubrey said, "Fair enough. Though I still don't think I'd be much help in the matter of selection. I didn't grow up with staff; I haven't the first idea how to choose them."

To Aubrey's relief, Lindsey seemed to accept this point, and the conversation returned to the more comfortable themes of Paris and painting.

~

CHAPTER TWO

After dinner they retired to Lindsey's bedroom, now called the master bedroom by the staff, though it was the same one Lindsey had through all the years since his departure from Eton.

It was also the same one in which Aubrey had introduced Lindsey to the delights of sodomy. Twice over.

At present, whilst Lindsey began undressing to change into his nightclothes, Aubrey found himself staring at the four-post bed. Thick golden ropes held back the heavy velvet curtains in deep crimson, and monstrous lion's paws as big as a man's skull formed the feet of the cherry-wood frame. Aubrey hadn't slept in this bed since...

Lindsey glanced over at him with curiosity.

"I was just thinking," Aubrey said, "of the last time we were here."

Lindsey looked around the room. As he did so, his bemused expression became a canny one, and by the time he returned to Aubrey, his eyes held a glint of mischief. "And what we did then?"

What they'd done, indeed. Aubrey had debauched Lindsey. Thoroughly.

"Shall we do it again?" Lindsey continued, echoing Aubrey's own want.

He stepped closer, and Aubrey took advantage of his proximity to pull him down by his cravat for a kiss. Lindsey laughed into his mouth. It took mere moments for Aubrey to steer him onto the bed, to divest them both of their garments, and to grab a jar of Vaseline from the washstand.

Some time afterward, Aubrey collapsed beside Lindsey, half on top of him as well as within him. Their legs tangled together as Aubrey wrapped his arms around Lindsey's chest and pulled himself flush with his spine, feeling Lindsey's shaking breaths rumble through his own ribcage. He kissed the nape of his neck, the hollow of his throat, the slope of his shoulder, tasting the salt of his sweat upon his tongue. Purest bliss flowed through his veins. Then Lindsey turned over in his arms to kiss him properly, and they lay entwined for who knew how many moments, utterly content.

"Lindsey," Aubrey murmured, not sure if his lover had fallen asleep.

"Yes?" came the whispered answer, along with Lindsey blindly stroking Aubrey's hair.

"What," Aubrey asked, grateful Lindsey couldn't see his scarlet cheeks in the dark, "is Icarus?"

It troubled Aubrey not to know something everyone else around him seemed to understand by instinct. Never mind that he knew more engineering than the lot of them put together. He hadn't dined with engineers. He'd dined with aristocrats and artists and found himself locked out of their cultural camaraderie. Not intentionally on their part, of course—except perhaps for Graves. But locked out nonetheless. Set apart and grasping at conversational straws in his efforts to keep up. He half-expected Lindsey to laugh at him for asking questions about something so apparently simple.

"Oh!" said Lindsey. "Greek myth. It's part of the tale of Theseus…"

Aubrey relaxed. He needn't have worried in the first place; Lindsey never objected to telling stories. Nor, for that matter, had Lindsey ever once teased Aubrey for not knowing something.

Lindsey's storytelling soon drowned out Aubrey's self-reproach. He listened as Lindsey spoke of a man who failed to sacrifice a bull to a god, a god who punished the man by making his wife fall in love with the bull, of the half-man, half-bull monster that resulted, the labyrinth built to contain it, the youths and maidens sacrificed to it, the champion who rose to end the sacrifice, the maiden who helped him navigate the labyrinth with a ball of string, the labyrinth-builder punished for the failure of his invention—which seemed to Aubrey rather unfair—and the labyrinth-builder's flight alongside his son. His literal flight, because the labyrinth-builder engineered feather-and-wax wings for himself and his son, Icarus.

"And if they flew too close to the sun," Lindsey explained, "the heat of the sun would melt the wax and the wings would break apart. So Daedalus warned Icarus not to fly so high. But then, of course, Icarus flew too high regardless, because it wouldn't be Greek if it weren't about punishing hubris, and his wings melted, and he fell down to earth and died."

"So Halloway wishes me to model as a boy who failed to follow simple instruction?" asked Aubrey.

Lindsey laughed. "I think it's more of an excuse to have a beautiful man covered only by half-melted wings."

Half-melted. Like Aubrey's face.

It wasn't the first time he'd been compared to a figure from Greek mythology. Ganymede, they used to call him. But Ganymede had been so beautiful that the lord of all gods had snatched him up to be his cup-bearer in the heavens.

Whereas half-melted Icarus had only himself to blame for his own destruction.

Lindsey put an arm around him, jolting him out of his self-pitying spiral. His long, elegant fingers traced Aubrey's cheek—the unburnt side—as he pressed a kiss to his lips.

Aubrey, relieved, kissed him back.

~

The next morning, Aubrey awoke first. Years of daily labour, first in the workhouse, then as a telegraph boy, then as a clerk, had altered his internal clock to rouse him before daybreak. He blinked blearily into the darkness for several confused moments before he recalled where he was and why. The presence of Lindsey, still sleeping beside him, precluded anything approaching unease.

Aubrey pressed a kiss to Lindsey's forehead, smoothed a few of his golden slumber-mussed curls, and quietly got out of bed to dress. Over the course of the months since the Rook Mill explosion, Aubrey and Charles had come to something of a silent understanding: Aubrey allowed Charles to continue looking after Lindsey in a more limited capacity, while Charles permitted Aubrey to look after himself as he'd always done.

He no longer had office hours to keep, but that was no reason to give in to sloth. The electrical conversion of the Rook Mill was still in the planning stages. Aubrey had those very plans in his possession and had brought them to the country house for opportunities such as this one. With no more noise than the slight shuffling of papers, he retrieved the plans and spread them over Lindsey's desk. He turned the gas lamp up just enough to see by, then sat down and settled in to the familiar work. Minutes ticked past, unheeded, into hours, and the bedroom gradually brightened with the growing dawn.

"What a marvellous day for riding!"

The sound of Lindsey's voice—so sudden and so clear—startled Aubrey out of his engineering reverie. He glanced up to find Lindsey had not only awoken, but risen from his bed, donned a robe, and crossed to the window to peer out at this unusually cloudless day.

More resplendent than the weather, to Aubrey at least, was the view of Lindsey himself. The silk robe hung off one shoulder, allowing a tantalising glimpse of his sweeping collarbone, his lean yet muscular chest, and his trim waist, with one jutting hipbone just visible before the robe's belt tucked everything else out of sight. The morning sunshine glowed through his golden curls, his blue eyes sparkled like the sea, and his winning smile beamed right back at the sky.

"Don't you think so?"

Aubrey, startled yet again out of a different yet no less compelling reverie, struggled to answer Lindsey's question. "I wouldn't know."

Lindsey turned his head to regard him with a quizzical expression.

"I don't ride," Aubrey reminded him.

"Oh," said Lindsey, colouring.

Aubrey hadn't meant to chide him, merely to state a practical fact. Born in an East London workhouse and having never spent more than a few days outside of a city, Aubrey hadn't possessed the means nor opportunity to learn how to ride a horse. Men of his station walked wherever they needed to go or took a train or omnibus if the distance were considerable. Horses pulled the omnibuses, as well as carts and hackney-cabs and any other wheeled conveyance in the street, but the only people Aubrey had ever seen on horseback were mounted police officers or the horse-guards. Even the wealthy typically rode within carriages rather than astride a saddle, at least in the city.

In the country, however, riding was a matter of course. Aubrey knew that much, despite his urban upbringing. The toffs he'd serviced in his earlier career had spoken freely, to each other if not to him, of the horses they kept and the horses they bought and the horses they rode in steeplechasing or fox-hunting. Little lordlings were often put in the saddle from the moment they could toddle along on foot, if not before. And Lindsey, Aubrey knew, had been no exception to that rule. A ripping sportsman, so his friends called him. He could ride neck-and-neck with the best of them.

Lindsey cleared his throat and added, somewhat bashfully, "The offer to learn still stands."

An offer Lindsey had made on Aubrey's first visit to the Wiltshire house, and one Aubrey had almost forgotten. In his defence, there'd been rather a lot going on besides touring the stables. Particularly a different sort of riding.

"An offer I'm still considering," Aubrey replied with a smile.

Lindsey crossed the room to bend down and kiss him. "How long have you been up?"

"Since five, or thereabouts." It had actually been quarter-to-five, but Aubrey didn't want to seem overly particular.

Lindsey's eyes widened. "Have you breakfasted?"

"Not yet."

This answer only seemed to alarm Lindsey further, prompting Aubrey to ask for the current time.

"Half-past ten," Lindsey replied. "You must be starving."

Aubrey, who knew what true starvation felt like, and that the dull gnawing in his gut was not yet it, acquiesced to Lindsey's conclusion, regardless.

~

In the breakfast room, Aubrey had supposed the conversation might turn towards Halloway's impending arrival, or the electrical conversion of Rook Mill, or Lindsey's own future wedding.

But Lindsey, levelling a considering look at Aubrey, said, "We should get you some riding clothes."

Aubrey, who had a piece of toast halfway to his mouth, lowered it back to his plate. He hadn't considered that riding required different clothes than mere pedestrianism. "Is that really necessary?"

Lindsey seemed surprised by the question. "Boots, certainly. And boots require breeches. At that point, you might as well have the whole kit."

Aubrey wished he knew how much riding boots cost. He knew the price of a decent pair of second- or third-hand ankle-high boots. But riding boots went far further up the leg, requiring much more material, which had to increase manufacturing costs. Furthermore, since only toffs rode horses, only toffs required riding boots, which meant the price of the product rose to meet the expected income of the customer. They wouldn't come cheap, of that much Aubrey felt certain. And that was just the boots. The whole kit, as Lindsey put it, could only cost more.

"You've already given me three new suits," Aubrey protested weakly. He wore one of those very suits now—the grey one. Lindsey had purchased it, along with a navy and a black, for Aubrey in the wake of the accident at Rook Mill. Aubrey, convalescing in hospital, hadn't had much say in it. By the time he discovered the gifts at Lindsey's house in Manchester, he could hardly refuse. For one, they'd all been made to order. For another, his one and only suit jacket had been destroyed by the same boiler explosion that melted his face.

That, and turning down Lindsey's gifts left him feeling just as guilty as receiving them. It resulted in a particularly heartbreaking expression coming over Lindsey's brow, dimming his natural smile and leaving him looking perfectly crestfallen. A heart of cold iron couldn't stand to disappoint Lindsey. Aubrey had no chance whatsoever.

The crestfallen expression had begun to creep into Lindsey's face now, though he made a game attempt at maintaining his sunny look. "Everyday and evening suits, certainly. But nothing suitable for riding."

Aubrey, unwilling to commit to the purchase of anything if he could find a more economical alternative, hesitated. He might not even like riding after all, and if so, anything made for him towards that purpose would be a total waste. "Could I not learn in an everyday suit?"

Lindsey looked him over. "I suppose..." His expression brightened. "And it would allow you to start without delay! Take advantage of this splendid weather. Get some exercise in, around Halloway's painting."

Aubrey tried not to show his panic at the sudden change in plan. It wasn't as though Lindsey were asking him to do anything outrageous. Plenty of people rode horses every day. And he had little else to occupy him here in the countryside. "Tomorrow, then?"

He could tell from Lindsey's bewildered blink that it'd been expected the riding lessons would begin today, but Aubrey needed at least another night's sleep to brace himself.

Lindsey quickly recovered from his initial bewilderment to beam at Aubrey. "Tomorrow it is."

~

CHAPTER THREE

Halloway arrived in the early afternoon. Lindsey had sent out the Althorp family carriage, along with a pair of strapping footmen, to retrieve him from the train station. These footmen proved essential, as Halloway arrived with a suitcase in each hand and a steamer trunk besides. Lindsey came to the foyer to greet his guest, but regrettably could not stay to do much more, as he had to dash off to the stables to prepare for Aubrey's impending riding lessons. Instead, Aubrey led Halloway—and the two footmen carrying the trunk between them—to his intended studio: the ballroom of the Wiltshire house.

Floor-to-ceiling windows formed the south-facing wall, bringing in sunshine from dawn to dusk. Equally tall mirrors covered the north-facing wall, doubling the sunlight in their reflection. Should such light prove insufficient, a chandelier worthy of an opera house glittered overhead. All combined to make the ballroom the brightest room in the whole house. Perfect conditions for painting, just as Lindsey had promised.

And a far cry from Halloway's rooms in the lodging-house he'd once shared with Aubrey. Though Halloway's rooms were much more commodious than Aubrey's garret, they hardly had enough room to turn around in amongst the easels, canvas, and countless papers, with sheets draped over furniture to create neutral backgrounds for models, windows wide open to let in as much air and sunshine as the streets of Manchester would allow—and the streets of Manchester allowed very little of the first and almost nothing of the second. Aubrey had only glimpsed Halloway's rooms through the doorway as Halloway, leaning against the doorframe with a cigarette balanced between two fingers, casually asked him to model, and offered him damned good money for it. Then, Aubrey had assumed it was a precursor to another sort of proposition, and, newly determined to live a respectable life as a clerk rather than a telegraph boy, politely but firmly declined. Halloway, to Aubrey's surprise, had taken the refusal in stride, thanked him for his time, and remained as friendly as any other neighbour in the lodging house. A good deal friendlier than the tract-writing Mr Brown, that much was certain.

Then Aubrey had met Lindsey, and through Lindsey met Graves, and through Graves found himself re-introduced to Halloway, and realised he might have been more right in his initial assumptions about the man than he thought. And Halloway still wanted to paint him.

Yet only after the boiler explosion at Rook Mill had burnt off half his face did Aubrey grow more amicable to the idea of modelling for Halloway. Aubrey wondered if Halloway resented him for waiting so long. If Halloway regretted missing the opportunity to capture the whole of Aubrey's apparently remarkable features. The face which had earned him the name of Ganymede amongst the toffs who hired him to perform less respectable services.

At present, Halloway did not appear in the least bit resentful or regretful. Indeed, he seemed downright chipper.

"Fantastic," he declared as he stepped into the ballroom, looking over the windows, mirrors, and chandeliers with approval. He set down his case and turned to direct the footmen carrying his trunk.

The trunk, once opened, revealed contents so tightly-packed and meticulously organised that it seemed Halloway had condensed his entire lodging-house studio into a single massive brick. Tarps, pulleys, easels, canvas, alongside several bizarre and unidentifiable bits and bobs—Halloway pulled an apparently-endless stream of objects out of it, and by the time the trunk was empty, it looked like its contents had exploded all across the ballroom.

With Aubrey's assistance, Halloway regathered the contents into neater piles in the corner of the room where the most concentrated light fell. One pile contained tarps and a great number of cushions Halloway had asked the footmen to commandeer from other rooms. The other held all of Halloway's artistic equipment, which included more mechanical elements than Aubrey had expected. He couldn't help appreciating the ingenuity of the engineering that allowed Halloway to turn what appeared to be a few scattered sticks, screws, and clamps into a full-fledged easel. Halloway then set a particular sketchbook upon the easel, and, looking between it and the pile of tarps and cushions, adjusted all accordingly until he achieved the desired positioning, distance, and proportions.

"Think you could lie comfortably on that?" Halloway asked, gesturing towards the resulting arrangement of cushions, which, along with the now-empty steamer trunk, lay underneath the draped tarps.

Aubrey agreed that he could, though something concerned him. He was, by his own admission, rather a new scholar to the myth of Icarus. Yet he couldn't help thinking that if Icarus had fallen upon such a soft pile of cushions and cloth, he'd have stood a very good chance of surviving his injuries. He brought this point up to Halloway, more carefully phrased, as he didn't wish his confusion to come across as criticism.

Far from appearing offended, Halloway plucked a sketchbook out of the chaos and began flipping through it with rapidity. Aubrey beheld page after page of rocky seascapes painted in watercolours. Halloway stopped at a particular painting of a craggy beach, with cliffs looming in the background, and held it up for Aubrey's inspection.

"The Amalfi Coast," he said by way of explanation. "But it should do well enough for the coast of the Icarian Sea."

"Ah," said Aubrey.

"As for the wings—" Halloway handed the first sketchbook off to Aubrey and picked up another. Flipping through its pages in turn revealed scores upon scores of birds, done in pencil, charcoal, and watercolour, laid out upon the ground in a wide variety of poses and angles, all quite deceased. "As you can see, we've plenty of pairs to choose from."

"You've been planning this for a while," Aubrey observed, unable to keep the ghost of a wry smile from his lips.

Halloway grinned freely in return. "Had to wait for the right model to become available."

Aubrey took the compliment in the spirit it was obviously intended. Though he couldn't help but wonder what Halloway would have done to secure the right model if Aubrey hadn't conveniently burned off half his own face.

Halloway, meanwhile, had discarded his jacket, rolled up his shirtsleeves, and set a sketchbook upon the easel, turned to a new page. As he opened his case to reveal tubes of paint, rows upon rows, along with long-handled brushes of varying widths and textures, he looked to Aubrey again. "Feel free to slip into something more comfortable."

It was far from the first time Aubrey had disrobed at another man's behest. It was, however, rather a new context for it. None of his former clientele had ever attempted to capture his appearance, all too wary of the consequences if their connexion should be discovered, and not wanting any possible proof of it, even as a keepsake.

Halloway had already returned to the tools of his trade, busy arranging his camp stool in front of his easel and putting his brushes and palette within easy reach.

Aubrey took advantage of the opportunity to shuck his garments, folding them up neat and quick, and shrugging on the silk dressing-gown Lindsey had given him. A soft breeze ghosted through the room. What, under normal circumstances, would've only made the hair on the back of his neck stand on end, now affected the hair all over him. He shivered.

"Cold?" Halloway enquired casually, glancing up from his work.

"Not too cold," Aubrey replied, desperate to save face and unable to account for how vulnerable he felt. He'd done this before. He'd done worse before, even. Though doing so in the broad light of day, and under the eyes of one he considered a friend, and in such a large room with an entire wall of windows...

Halloway looked him over, then put down his sketchbook and approached. "Could you lie down here?"

Aubrey followed where he indicated. He felt beyond awkward as he lowered himself onto the pile.

Mercifully, Halloway continued to speak to him as matter-of-factly as if he'd remained clothed. "Could you put your arm up under your head, and stretch out your hand—yes, just so—and drop your shoulder so your other arm bends over your side—perfect—and if you could turn your hips towards me..."

This last directive brought a hint of crimson to Aubrey's cheeks.

24

He contorted his body as instructed, regardless.

"Excellent," declared Halloway. Then, to Aubrey's infinite relief, he pulled out a bed-sheet and draped it over Aubrey's body in such a way as to obfuscate that which produced the most embarrassment, though it obscured little else.

"We'll start with an hour," Halloway announced. "Then see how you feel. Let me know if any limbs fall asleep in the meantime."

Aubrey assented, and Halloway returned to his easel to begin sketching in earnest.

An awkward silenced descended upon the ballroom. Only the gentle scuffing of pencil against parchment filled the air. Aubrey's mind raced, wondering how his naked flesh looked from Halloway's perspective: the swirling, pink-and-white burns running down the right side of his body, covering his face from temple to jawline; stretching from his half-melted ear to the corner of his mouth; running down the outer edge of his arm from triceps to hand; splashing over the side of his ribcage, marking the ribs he'd broken when the boiler explosion flung him across the mill yard and knocked him unconscious against the cobblestones. He struggled to force his mind down other, less painful avenues, not wanting to spend a full hour dwelling upon his own ugliness.

"How do you like the country?" Halloway asked.

The question jolted Aubrey out of his thoughts, much to his relief. "It's peaceful. Quiet, I suppose."

"So they say," Halloway replied, his pencil dashing over the page all the while. His gaze remained on Aubrey's body as he spoke, but his expression lacked the lechery Aubrey had experienced from other voyeurs. He looked upon Aubrey as Aubrey himself looked upon machines; contemplative, curious, his eyes tracing form in search of function. It seemed Halloway engineered images in much the same way Aubrey engineered electricity. "Too quiet, sometimes. I find it difficult to fall asleep out here. But the air's much fresher."

Aubrey agreed, and added, "Do you come out to the country often?"

"When the London season is done with," said Halloway. "Graves won't leave the city before then. And there's little point going away without him. Though lately he's preferred the Continent to the country. That's how I managed to get in those Italian seascapes."

Aubrey, who'd never been to the Continent, found he had little to say upon the subject. "Do you like it?"

"Italy? Or holidaying with Graves?" Halloway gave wry smile, though his gaze remained upon Aubrey's legs, which he measured out by holding his pencil up at arm's length. "I like both. Though there's nothing quite like the English countryside."

Aubrey thought of Lindsey riding across that very countryside now.

"Will you be joining Sir Lindsey this afternoon?" Halloway asked, as if he could read Aubrey's thoughts. "Riding, I mean."

"I will," Aubrey admitted. "Lindsey's determined to teach me how."

Halloway stopped sketching and looked up into Aubrey's eyes rather than over his body. "You've never ridden before?"

Aubrey coloured. "I have not."

"Not even in Hyde Park?" Halloway asked.

Aubrey, who'd only ever visited the city parks by night, found himself caught between embarrassment and amusement, and struggled to keep his composure as he replied, "No."

Aubrey wondered if Halloway would go on to ask about the Horse Guards—they had something in common with telegraph boys, after all—but either Halloway knew better than to confound similar back-alley habits with similar equestrian pursuits, or he didn't realise the Horse Guards rivalled the Royal Navy in their reputation for sodomy. He returned to his sketching regardless, as coolly as if he'd never stopped.

"Should be exciting, then," he observed.

Aubrey tried not to take the offhand comment as a personal dig. "Do you ride?"

"Not often," Halloway confessed. "Not much opportunity whilst I'm in Manchester."

"But Lord Graves must," Aubrey said before he could think better of it.

"Indeed, he must," Halloway echoed. "His father keeps a renowned stable. Anything his father approves of, however, Graves must make a show of renouncing. So he doesn't ride as often as I rather think he'd like. When he does ride, though, it must be upon the prettiest steed and at neck-or-nothing speed across the countryside. Nothing stirs him up quite like a fox hunt."

Aubrey hoped Lindsey didn't expect him to participate in blood sport. It didn't seem like Lindsey, soft-hearted as he was, to delight in such pointless slaughter—though he was a fair shot when it came to birding. "Do you ride with Lord Graves, then?"

Halloway laughed. "As if I could keep up!"

~

Lindsey considered himself on good terms with the gamekeeper, the master of hounds, the grooms in the stables, the butler, Mr Hudson—and, of course, with Charles. But he'd not often had reason to consult with the female staff. Rowena had been mistress of the Althorp household since the age of fifteen. And as far as Lindsey could tell, she ran it as tight as any ship in Her Majesty's navy.

Of course, she didn't do so alone. She had the assistance of the housekeeper, Mrs Sheffield.

And thus, whilst Aubrey modelled for Halloway's painting, Lindsey went up to the library and asked Charles to send for Mrs Sheffield to meet him there. He'd hardly opened *The Pall Mall Gazette* before she arrived.

A strong-jawed woman of middling age, Mrs Sheffield appeared unchanged since Lindsey had last seen her, he knew not how many years ago. Her dress, starched and ironed to rival any officer's uniform, looked as if plucked out of a photograph from several decades before. In her typical brusque manner, yet nevertheless deferential, she asked, "How may I be of service, Sir Lindsey?"

"Miss Althorp has charged me with selecting staff to bring into the Manchester household."

If Mrs Sheffield found this out of the ordinary, she hid it very well. Lindsey supposed Rowena had occasion to give her far more outlandish orders in all the years since she took control of the chatelaine.

"She thought," Lindsey continued, "I might find at least a girl-of-all-work and a cook. Is there anyone you'd particularly recommend?"

After a moment's consideration, Mrs Sheffield replied, "I should think any of our girls would be well-suited to the position of parlour maid. But, with your leave, I shall ask which of them have an interest in a change of scene. As for the cook, I'm loathe to spare Mrs Goode..."

"Nor would I ask it of you," Lindsey replied in perfect solemnity.

Though he would miss the comfort of Mrs Goode's culinary prowess.

"However," Mrs Sheffield went on, "I may persuade her to leave go of one of her kitchen-maids. They've all trained up under her, and with the opportunity, will doubtless rise to the occasion."

"Splendid!" said Lindsey. Then, as a spark of inspiration struck him, he added, "Would it be possible for one such kitchen-maid to practice for her new role for the duration of our stay in the country?"

Mrs Sheffield concurred with his plan and, with a dignified curtsy, departed to carry out her orders.

Lindsey spent another moment entertaining himself with what his sister would think of his brilliant scheme, then finished with what he considered the interesting bits of *The Pall Mall Gazette* and moved on to *The Strand*. In the midst of a literary tour through the establishment of one Mr Doyle, the entrance of Charles interrupted Lindsey's reading.

"Mrs Sheffield," said Charles, "has consulted with Mrs Goode and they believe Miss Murphy will suit our purposes. In a related matter, luncheon is served."

~

The modelling continued until shortly before noon, when Halloway set down the tools of his trade, cracked his knuckles, and announced himself famished. Aubrey dressed again and joined Halloway in returning to the breakfast room. There they found luncheon laid out upon the table, and Lindsey already at its head.

"We're trying out a new cook," he explained as Aubrey and Halloway took their seats upon either side of him. "Miss Murphy is eager to prove herself."

From what Aubrey could judge of the quails and watercress, lamb cutlets with peas, and lemon-water ice, Miss Murphy had proved herself ten times over.

After luncheon, Halloway assured Aubrey he had plenty to work with from his sketches, and Aubrey, without any excuse remaining, finally conceded it might be time to go out to the stables. Lindsey retreated upstairs to don his riding attire. Halloway returned to the ballroom to continue his composition.

Which left Aubrey quite alone in the enormous emptiness of the country house.

And yet, whilst in Wiltshire, he could never truly call himself alone.

Even as he slipped out of the breakfast room, he espied out of the corner of his eye two footmen on their way to clean up after the gentlemen's meal. A wash of shame overcame him as he considered what sort of mess he might have left behind; he did his able best to conduct himself in a tidy fashion, but nevertheless he couldn't help thinking what the footmen might say between themselves. Endless comments about his appetite, his manners, whether he had left too much or too little food upon his plate, how his efforts at dirtying as few dishes as possible marked him out as a rustic unaccustomed to fine dining, or what they must think of him daring to sit at their master's right hand—all ran through Aubrey's mind in a closed circuit, no matter how he tried to wrench that particular train of thought off its track.

As such, he took an impulsive left turn down a corridor to avoid passing them and found himself in a part of the house he did not recognise. A long hallway of identical doors stretched out before him, ending in a crossway.

Aubrey, with a final glance over his shoulder at the way he'd come, plunged down the hallway. He wished he had the materials to solve the problem mathematically—a piece of chalk to mark the walls, for example, so he might make full use of Trémaux's method. In the absence of chalk, he supposed he must treat the house as a labyrinth rather than a true maze. To this end, he raised his left hand to the wall until his fingertips grazed its pristine surface, and continued on his way, keeping contact with the wall as he went, with allowances for the doors which dotted its length. When he came to the crossway, he turned left, maintaining his hand on the wall all the while. This brought him into another hall of doors, ending in a pair of double doors flung wide, through which he recognised the grand entryway of the house, its sweeping staircase stretching diagonally across the opening.

However, his victory in coming so soon to the end of his predicament proved short-lived. For as he strode forth, he caught a snatch of conversation, growing louder and louder as he approached the foyer.

"—ask Mrs Sheffield?"

"She'll only tell me I'm being foolish. Can't you just trade rounds with me? I'm half-dead of fright as it is!"

The two young women's voices drifted out from a door halfway down the hall, just cracked ajar. Aubrey, already determined to push past it to reach the safety of the foyer, slowed at the mention of fright. He glanced through the crack of the door as he passed. Some manner of sitting room lay within, with sofas and settees and armchairs scattered about, and two maids in identical black-and-white uniforms, one kneeling by the fireplace to black the grate, the other standing by with her arms crossed over herself in a protective gesture, shoulders hunched, bent down to speak to the working girl.

"What's there to be frightened of?" asked the girl at the grate, not pausing her task. A lock of dark hair fell out from under her white cap, and she tucked it back behind her ear without ceremony. She spoke low, her words collected and calm, with a slight lilting accent— Welsh, Aubrey thought.

"What's to be frightened—?" the upright girl echoed in disbelief. "You've seen him! That face!"

Even as he'd listened, Aubrey had scolded himself for his foolish vanity in supposing the word 'him' referred to himself. Yet the final words removed all possible ambiguity. Hot shame surged through his cheeks, burnt and unburnt alike, flaring up the back of his neck and scorching his ears.

"It gives me horrors, it does!" the upright girl went on. "I can't bear to go into the master chambers alone—what if he should walk in behind my back, and I turn away from the mantle to see—!" She cut herself off, shuddering. "All half-melted, like a wax figure come to life! I'd rather scour pots in the kitchen than risk seeing—"

"I'll do it," said the girl at the grate.

The frightened girl appeared as shocked as Aubrey felt at her interruption. The girl at the grate had never yet looked up from her blacking.

"You will?" the frightened girl asked, as much suspicious as hopeful.

The girl at the grate looked up at last. She turned away from Aubrey as she did, and he couldn't see her face, but from her tone, he supposed she'd fixed the frightened girl with a severe expression. "So long as you never call such a face a horror again."

The frightened girl blinked at her. "But—!"

"I don't care what you think of it," said the girl at the grate. She pushed herself up from her kneeling pose, and stood at least a head shorter than her fellow maid. "I don't want to hear it."

Her voice remained low and level throughout, revealing no touch of anger or scorn, and yet so stern as to brook no argument.

The frightened girl looked as if she had a great deal more to say on the subject, but shut her mouth with a nod.

The working girl bent to the grate again to pick up her bucket and brush. In doing so, her face turned towards the doorway.

Aubrey ducked away from the opening lest she catch sight of him and escaped down the hallway—reflecting bitterly as he went that he should have gone on ahead in the first place, and never stopped to eavesdrop at all.

~

Aubrey had toured the stables just once before, on his initial visit to the Wiltshire house, the very same occasion when Lindsey first proposed riding lessons. Now, Aubrey found them much the same as then; warm, bright, smelling of horseflesh and hay, full of handsome steeds and handsome grooms.

Over the course of his time with Lindsey, Aubrey had learnt that most households hired footmen on the basis of their height first and their handsome features second, with capability forming a more distant third. Thus, he knew the presence of so many tall and well-formed young men in livery was not so unusual as he'd first supposed.

However, most households didn't use the same hiring requirements for the grooms or the gardeners or any other place in the staff a man might fill.

Rowena, in her efforts to channel her brother's interest, had.

And so every man in the Wiltshire house besides Aubrey stood over six feet tall and had, at the very least, extraordinarily symmetrical features, if not striking ones.

Aubrey, with his small frame and his half-melted face, felt rather like an imp amongst angels. Any moment the grooms would realise he didn't belong and swoop down upon him to toss him out of their Heaven.

But, of course, they did no such thing. Though Aubrey did catch a couple of sidelong glances out of the corner of his eye. They didn't look at his face. Not the whole of it. They looked at his burn scars, and then quickly away.

Aubrey turned his attention to the horses. These, at least, didn't stare at his scars. He wasn't sure they could stare, what with their eyes on opposite sides of their heads. They hardly seemed to notice him at all. Just kept on pawing the stable floor, munching straw, shaking their heads, occasionally snorting. They might kill him with their powerful muscles and massive hooves, but they wouldn't judge his appearance.

"Aubrey!"

Aubrey whirled at the sound of Lindsey's voice, lowered out of respect for their surroundings, but nonetheless joyful.

Lindsey stood at the entrance to the stables. Sun streamed through the open doors to bathe him in an heroic glow, turning the golden curls spilling out from beneath his top hat into an ethereal halo. A well-tailored coat clung to his slender waist, drawing Aubrey's gaze in and down to the fawn-coloured breeches. These, so tight Lindsey appeared sewn into them, gave a splendid view of his lean, sinewy thighs and slid straight down into his tall black boots. The boots, polished to a gleaming sheen, had a heel just high enough to accentuate the elegant curve of his calves. This, then, was a man in full riding costume, and what a marvellous effect it had.

Aubrey realised he'd been staring, swallowed, and said, "Good morning."

Lindsey grinned. "Have you chosen your steed?"

"Not yet," Aubrey admitted. "Have you?"

"Indeed I have! Come and see."

Aubrey joined Lindsey in the doorway. Lindsey gestured out into the stable yard, and a little way beyond to a particular circle of fenced-in turf. Within this enclosure stood an enormous beast, with hooves broader than Aubrey's skull, and a head as long as his torso. A handsome groom held its bridle—a groom who either had a surfeit of courage or did not value his own life too highly, by Aubrey's reckoning.

"This is Bellerophon," Lindsey declared, gazing on the creature with as much fond tenderness as if it were a puppy.

"How tall...?" Aubrey started to ask, then trailed off as he realised it was a stupid question. The answer, obviously, was too tall. The beast tossed its head well above Lindsey and all the grooms.

"Eighteen hands at the withers," Lindsey proudly announced.

Aubrey wondered how to convert hands to feet and inches, and furthermore, where exactly on the animal one might find the withers. Its shoulders towered over him, that much he knew for certain.

"Fletcher thinks Parsival might do for you to start on," Lindsey added.

Aubrey, half-afraid to ask just how many hands tall were Parsival's withers, turned away from the mighty aspect of Bellerophon to regard the approach of one of the grooms who'd stolen glances at him just moments earlier.

Fletcher, a tall young man with sandy hair and moustache, nodded briskly to his employer and to Aubrey in turn. Lindsey bid Fletcher show them Parsival's stall, and Fletcher led the way down to the other end of the stables, past many more giant beasts at rest.

"Parsival," Fletcher said when they reached the appropriate stall.

Aubrey peered up at the horse. He supposed its dapple grey coat pleasing to the eye. And its ears seemed to swivel with less unnerving frequency than those of its companions. Its large brown eyes roved over the three men. Then it ducked its head—Aubrey fought the urge to jump back—and gently butted its nose against Fletcher's chest.

Fletcher, with perfect *sangfroid*, pulled a chunk of carrot from his pocket and held it out to Parsival in a flat palm. Parsival's maw opened to reveal a row of teeth like chisels, each blade wider than Aubrey's thumb and about as long. The enormous flapping lips picked up the treat, and with a crunch like cracking bone, the carrot vanished down Parsival's gullet. Fletcher gave a gentle pat to the horse's muscular neck.

"Gelding," Lindsey offered up in answer to Aubrey's many, many unspoken questions. "Sixteen hands."

Smaller than Bellerophon, at least. Though it certainly didn't look small up close. Aubrey, no innate judge of horseflesh, could do little more than nod his assent to the groom's choice.

Fletcher appeared sceptical. "Beggin' your pardon, sir, but may I see your boots?"

Aubrey, reminded none-too-fondly of being asked to present his personal effects for inspection at the workhouse, plucked at the knees of his trousers to pull the hems up away from his boots, raising each foot in turn and twisting it to show Fletcher the sole. Even in the soft light of the stables, every scuff and scratch stood out like lightning against stormy skies.

"You've got a heel at least," Fletcher conceded. "They'll do well enough to keep your feet in the stirrups for today."

Without further ado, Fletcher took the horse out of the stall and, assisted by his fellow grooms, began tacking him up. Lindsey, apparently content to leave his servants to their work, returned to the stable yard, and Aubrey followed him.

"It might," Aubrey said in a low voice after touching Lindsey's arm to get his attention, "assist me in understanding how to go about horse-riding if I had a fresh example in my mind."

Lindsey required no further prompting to stride out into the paddock towards proud Bellerophon. He walked right up to the beast's left side, put his hands upon its back, slid one foot into the stirrup, then leapt into the air and swung his leg out over the saddle in one fluid motion, coming down into a seat as easy and comfortable as if he were perched in his favourite chair, the reins already caught up in his hands, smooth and effortless.

At some secret signal, Bellerophon started forward, his gait resolving into what even Aubrey could recognise as a trot. Lindsey gracefully rose and fell in the saddle in tandem with his steed's movements, as easily balanced as if he walked upon his own two legs.

Aubrey watched the whole proceedings from his perch against a fence-post. The stunning display absorbed all his attention so thoroughly that he didn't notice Fletcher's approach until the man spoke.

"He's an able sportsman, is Sir Lindsey," Fletcher declared with no small amount of admiration in his tone.

Aubrey certainly agreed, yet something about the praise gave him pause. Fletcher, like all the rest of the grooms, and every other male servant in the house—apart from the butler, Mr Hudson—had been hired by Rowena with very specific hopes in mind. To wit, that should Lindsey's nature overwhelm him, he would find a relatively safe outlet amongst the staff. Not only was every man on the property tall and strikingly handsome, but, to hear Graves tell it, had also been chosen for his predilection to respond favourably to untoward advances from his employer.

Before now, Aubrey had assumed this merely meant Rowena had gone out of her way to hire a full staff of sodomites. But the admiration in Fletcher's tone as he praised Lindsey's skills as a sportsman shone new light upon the situation. Perhaps the staff were more than inclined to react well to indecent proposals. Perhaps they were expecting them. Perhaps they'd even hoped for them.

Until Aubrey came along.

For all he knew, any man on staff at the Wiltshire house had banked on improving his position in life through becoming the chosen favourite. Then, in a sequence of events absolutely no one could have predicted, Lindsey had won a mill in a card game, encountered a particular lowly clerk at said mill, and had given his heart over to him at first sight. Aubrey knew well how unspeakably lucky he was to have met Lindsey. Yet he also knew how their meeting had thrown a wrench into everyone else's plans for the baronet.

Everyone's plans, quite possibly including his staff's.

"Ought to see him jump," Fletcher added, drawing Aubrey out of his uncomfortable musings. "Fence, beck, stones—he'll throw his heart over any obstacle."

Fletcher looked as if he would speak on, but then Lindsey's circuit around the paddock brought him past where they stood, drawing their attention.

Lindsey tipped his hat to them as he trotted past. His broad smile bespoke an invitation as loud as any speech. *Join me?*

Aubrey dearly wished to do so. Lindsey's infectious enthusiasm boded well. And it'd be nice to share in something Lindsey found so enjoyable.

But when he thought of how his efforts at learning would compare to Lindsey's natural ease, he felt a cold lump of dread in his gullet. The grooms would doubtless receive quite a show from Aubrey's failed attempts to master as an adult what other men had mastered as children.

To say nothing of the horses themselves. Aubrey tried not to show it, but the close proximity of so many very large animals inspired no small amount of anxiety within him. He was an engineer; he worked with machines. Beautifully reliable machines that did what they were told. And even these—a boiler, in particular—had quite literally blown up in his face. He didn't like to dwell on what harm a wild and unpredictable animal might do.

A gruff snort behind him announced the arrival of one such

animal; Parsival, bridled and saddled and ready to wreak havoc upon Aubrey's person. Fletcher stepped up to take the reins from the other groom and lead Parsival into the paddock, just as Lindsey rode Bellerophon out of it.

Lindsey brought his steed over to stand before Aubrey. Aubrey found himself stumbling backward from the beast, whose nose hung level with Aubrey's forehead, and spread just as broad.

"Ready to give it a try?" Lindsey asked, bright as ever.

Aubrey forced a smile. "Ready as I'll ever be."

Lindsey dismounted in a single fluid movement and took up Fletcher's old post by the fence to watch.

Keenly feeling the pressure of Lindsey's eyes upon him, as well as the eyes of all the grooms, Aubrey entered the paddock.

"Nervous, sir?" Fletcher said as he approached. "Don't be."

The words implied comfort, but the tone spoke otherwise. Aubrey levelled a questioning look at the groom.

"If you're nervous," Fletcher warned, "the horse'll spook."

Aubrey couldn't think of a sentence more inclined to make a person nervous.

"Stand here, sir," Fletcher bid him, motioning to the left-hand side of the horse, near the saddle.

Aubrey moved to the indicated position.

"Put your left foot into the stirrup," Fletcher continued. "Grab onto the saddle here, and some mane there—exactly so, sir—and spring off with your right leg."

Aubrey, thinking back to Lindsey's swift and sure mounting, attempted to imitate it. He bounced off the ground—and fell immediately back on his heel, hopping around on one leg to regain balance. Parsival didn't take kindly to all this nonsense and took a few uneasy steps away from his would-be rider, forcing Aubrey to yank his left foot out of the stirrup and stumble backwards to stay upright.

"Good effort, sir," Fletcher said dispassionately, looking at the horse rather than at Aubrey. He caught up the reins—Aubrey rather wished he'd done that from the start, rather than let the horse walk away from him—and steered Parsival back into position. "Shall we try again?"

Aubrey, not one to give up so quickly, tried again. This time Parsival stayed in place. So did Aubrey, hopping up and down on one leg as he tried, and failed, to pull himself up into the saddle, over and over again.

A hand on his arm stopped him. Aubrey turned, expecting Fletcher. Instead he found Lindsey.

"If I might make a suggestion," said Lindsey, whose face still bore a gentle smile. "It's as much or more about pushing down with the left leg, as it is springing from the right. Much more so than pulling with the arms."

Aubrey knew Lindsey meant well. Lindsey always meant well. But knowing this didn't make him feel any less humiliated. Nor did it prevent his flaming cheeks from touting said humiliation all across the stable yard for every groom to behold—indeed, to Aubrey, the heat of his own blush felt so intense he would have sworn any maid in the house could perceive it, if she happened to peer out of an upstairs window at that moment. He wondered for one bitter instant why Lindsey couldn't have offered such helpful wisdom before he ever attempted to mount Parsival.

Yet such bitterness couldn't long survive under the benevolent rays of Lindsey's hopeful smile.

Aubrey withheld a sigh, thanked him, and turned back to the waiting saddle. Again, he put his left hand upon the horse's mane. Once more, he put his right hand upon the saddle. He slid his left foot into the stirrup, and gave one last valiant attempt at springing from his right. As his right foot left the ground, he threw his weight onto his left and forced it to unbend, pushing him further up, up, up—and very nearly over.

But not quite.

Having vaulted into the air, he then attempted to throw his right leg out across the saddle, as he'd seen Lindsey do with such ease and grace. Whether it was due to his own inexperience, or simply because his legs were not near so long as Lindsey's, Aubrey found he did not possess anything like the same ease or grace. As such, his right leg, rather than coming down on the opposite side of his steed and sliding smoothly into the waiting stirrup, came down upon the horse's backside.

Parsival, to his credit, neither bucked nor reared at this alarming development. But he did stamp his hoof in protest, and this was enough to send Aubrey sprawling backward. His prior dismounts were pure elegance compared to how he now flailed through the air and fell down upon his arse in the dirt.

A single bark of laughter echoed through the stable yard. Aubrey glanced 'round him to see which groom had so forgot himself as to vocalise the fun he had at his master's engineer's expense, only to find the grooms stone-faced, and Lindsey with one hand clamped over his mouth to muffle any further escaping mirth. His blue eyes danced with delight, even as Aubrey stared up at him in disbelief.

"Sorry!" Lindsey gasped when he finally recovered himself. He started to offer Aubrey his arm, but Aubrey had already scrambled to his feet unassisted.

"Might help to have something to stand on, sir," Fletcher suggested. "So you wouldn't have to jump so high. Overturned bucket should do the trick."

The thought of standing on a bucket to climb into the saddle sent a fresh wave of shame through Aubrey. Lindsey hadn't stood on a bucket. Then again, Lindsey stood far taller than Aubrey—indeed, far taller than most men, though Aubrey found it difficult to remember this fact whilst surrounded by a stable-full of grooms who all stood eye-to-eye with Lindsey.

Still, even Aubrey had to concede that it was a little much to attempt an unassisted jump over an obstacle almost as tall as himself, without even the benefit of a running start. The physics of the problem simply didn't work out.

"Here," said Lindsey.

The sound of his voice drew Aubrey out of his mental calculations. He turned to find Lindsey in a peculiar pose. Lindsey stood beside Parsival, just behind the saddle, with his hands held out in front of him, palms up, fingers interlaced. It took Aubrey a moment to recognise the meaning of the gesture. Once he did, he blushed anew.

Lindsey intended for Aubrey to step on his hands, and thus raise him up onto the horse.

Aubrey wondered how it appeared to all the grooms, to see a baronet—their employer—holding out his hands for some workhouse brat's boot to stamp upon. He came very near to refusing.

But the apologetic smile upon Lindsey's lips and the clear blue honesty of his eyes melted all of Aubrey's obstinacy away.

Once again, Aubrey approached Parsival, with his face towards the horse's head and his back towards Lindsey. He put his hands on the mane and saddle and slipped his left foot into the stirrup. He glanced over his shoulder, then, at Lindsey's nod, jumped from his right leg whilst pushing off with his left.

For one horrible second, he hung suspended in the air.

Then Lindsey caught his heel.

In the space of a blink, Aubrey felt himself pulled up and pushed over. He hurried to match Lindsey's movements, lest his sacrificial efforts be in vain. His leg cleared the horse's back—his seat came down upon the saddle—

And he was up.

Aubrey blinked in astonishment at his new vantage point. None so high as riding atop an omnibus, no. Still, far taller than he'd ever stood in all his four-and-twenty years. It had a rather dizzying effect, not helped by the horse shifting underneath him, as if he sat atop a buoy on the ocean, which to Aubrey made his steed no less disconcerting from above than from below. To say nothing of how it felt as if one wrong move would make him as much of a gelding as Parsival.

"Steady," said Fletcher.

Whether he spoke to the man or the horse, Aubrey couldn't say. But as he glanced around to ascertain, he saw Lindsey gazing upon him with a look equal parts wonder and triumph. Aubrey dared a smile at him and found it returned tenfold.

"Shoulders down, sir," said Fletcher.

The abrupt reminder of his own terrible posture brought Aubrey's elevated mood crashing back down to reality. Aubrey rolled his shoulders, stiff muscles straining with protest against such rough treatment. Though he kept his shoulders back and his head erect whilst walking—the concept of external poise reflecting internal moral character having been drilled into him from a young age—he shared the bad habit of most office workers, in that once he sat down, he tended to hunch over his task.

This same hunch did him no favours upon horseback. He rolled his shoulders again, endeavouring to keep them down despite the burning sensation. Doing so required him to suck in his gut and hollow out his lower back—positioning which felt even less secure in the saddle then it did on the ground. His arms hung loose, and for lack of anything else to grasp, he clutched the horse's mane in both hands.

"Very good, sir," Fletcher said, his tone perfunctory. "If you'll just lower your heels."

Aubrey, confused, glanced down at his boots. At present, he had both in their respective stirrups, their toes pointed squarely at the ground. Common sense told him if he lowered his heels, said boots would then slip backwards out of these same stirrups, and his position in the saddle would become still more precarious. He wondered, briefly, if Fletcher were playing some sort of prank.

Yet Fletcher appeared as impassive as ever. And surely, Aubrey reasoned upon reflection, even if the groom did wish him the worst, he wouldn't dare commit any sabotage under Lindsey's nose.

Aubrey slowly raised his toes and lowered his heels. To his surprise, his boots did not slip out of place. On the contrary, his arches braced against the stirrup all the more securely.

Fletcher nodded. "Just so, sir. And if you'll bring your thighs in line with the saddle flaps…"

Doing so required some creative unbending of Aubrey's knees, which had up to this point remained elevated, as if he were sitting in a chair. But once corrected in accordance with Fletcher's instruction, Aubrey found his legs fell into a loose and natural grip of the saddle. It did, however, require him to transfer his weight from his seat to his fork, which did not improve the sensation of imperiled stones. And remembering every aspect of this new and unfamiliar posture— shoulders down, hollow-backed, lowered heels, aligned thighs— required a great deal of concentration. The strain of his muscles in every direction didn't help matters.

"With your permission, sir," said Fletcher, "I'll lead him around at a walk."

Aubrey, despite his best instincts, nodded.

Fletcher turned away. Parsival followed. Despite their slow and steady pace, every powerful stride rolled up through the beast's body to the saddle. Aubrey found himself swaying from side to side with each step, which only made his precarious posture all the more difficult to maintain. Still, he didn't slip out of the saddle—despite feeling very much as if he were about to do so at any moment.

Parsival completed the circuit around the paddock, bringing them all back around to where Lindsey stood watching.

"How d'you find it so far?" Lindsey called up to him.

Aubrey felt his own smile growing sincere to match Lindsey's. "I rather like being tall."

~

CHAPTER FOUR

Aubrey spent the whole of the afternoon on horseback. By the time they broke for dinner, he felt rather accomplished—though Fletcher had yet to give him the reins. As he sat down to dinner with Lindsey and Halloway, he had the satisfying burn of a job well done in his shoulders and thighs.

By the end of dinner, everything ached.

His neck and shoulders burned from his forcing them to assume a position that, while technically correct and healthful, still felt absolutely unnatural. His spine had stretched and compacted in ways which could be charitably described as uncomfortable, and which he thought would best be described with language unfitting to his surroundings. His muscles fared no better, feeling to him as if someone had tied them in knots and set them on fire. His hip-joints felt as if dislocated and inexpertly re-attached; they seemed to grind in their sockets. Every inch of flesh on his legs burned down to the bone, from his thighs to his ankles. His skin stood in no better shape than his muscles, as his loose trouser legs pinched by the saddle had chafed his knees and inner thighs raw, and he staggered rather than walked up the stairs to Lindsey's bedroom after dinner.

"Are you feeling quite the thing?" Lindsey asked once the bedroom door had closed behind them.

"I'm fine," Aubrey mumbled. "Just a bit stiff."

He rubbed the back of his neck as he spoke, hoping to alleviate some of the tension. Lindsey reached up to aid in his efforts. Two soft hands with long, clever fingers worked far better than Aubrey's half-hearted one-handed attempt, and Aubrey let his arm drop to his side, just as his head dropped onto Lindsey's collar with a groan.

Lindsey laughed. His fingers slipped beneath Aubrey's lapels. Aubrey pulled back just enough to allow Lindsey to divest him of his jacket.

"A hot bath might do you good," Lindsey murmured into his ear as he unbuttoned his waistcoat.

"Don't think I've ever had a hot bath before," Aubrey mused aloud.

Lindsey looked up sharp. "Never?"

Aubrey coloured. Most days he made do with a stand-up wash like everyone else—which Lindsey well knew—but evidently the lack of baths still required explanation. "Went to the plunge pool in the public baths a few times with the other telegraph boys, but it's never hot. Or private." He didn't know which aspect felt more humiliating: the reminder of his sordid past or the revelation of his own inexperience.

Lindsey didn't seem to take offence to either. He simply smiled. "Well, then, you're in for a treat."

Aubrey heartily agreed, though he felt too exhausted to do much to assist Lindsey in getting him there. Lindsey set aside his waistcoat and peeled off his shirt, then undid his braces and gently pushed Aubrey down to sit on the bed so he might untie his boots. He worked with equal parts efficiency and tenderness, his skilful fingers tracing caresses over his calves as he unhooked the garters holding up his stockings. In between divesting Aubrey of his trousers and undershirt, Lindsey even found time to steal a kiss. Such attentions left Aubrey more relaxed than otherwise, so that when Lindsey threw a silk dressing gown over his shoulders and guided him towards the bathroom, he felt perfectly content to follow.

Aubrey had seen the bathroom before on his visits to the Wiltshire house. He'd had a private breakdown in it on the morning after his first night with Lindsey. Even then, he'd taken note of the extravagant amenities, not only in the marble surroundings but in the plumbing itself. Indoor taps, running hot water as well as cold, were an incredible luxury for anyone, even those of Lindsey's class. Through conversational asides and idle chatter over the past few months, Aubrey discovered how such marvels came to pass.

The Wiltshire house had undergone significant renovations over the past decade, at Rowena's behest. From what Aubrey gleaned from Lindsey, it was she who required indoor bathing facilities attached to her bedroom suite. And, since it would hardly be fair to deny her brother the same privilege, she made the case to their father for the addition of a bathroom to Lindsey's suite, too. And if the children had baths, the father might as well, so she persuaded Sir Geoffrey to install plumbing throughout the house. It had taken many years and considerable expense, but the end result seemed well worth the effort. No servants had to haul pots of boiling water upstairs for a bath in the Wiltshire house. The pipes did all the work.

At present, Aubrey watched as Lindsey turned the tub's faucets, and the pipes rattled to life. Water gushed from the tap—Lindsey let it run over his hand to test the result and adjusted the faucets accordingly—followed shortly by steam. Truly a marvel of engineering; Aubrey couldn't help feeling impressed.

Then Lindsey's hands descended upon his shoulders and gently slipped off the silk dressing gown, leaving Aubrey exposed. He shivered despite the steam.

Lindsey, hardly more decent in just his shirtsleeves and with his topmost buttons undone, took Aubrey's arm to support him as he stepped into the bath.

Even whilst distracted by his own efforts to keep his balance on the slippery marble and wet enamel, Aubrey couldn't deny the sheer relief he felt as he slid under the water. It came up to his shoulders, the water level rising with the added volume of his body—he couldn't help thinking of Archimedes. No wonder Rowena had petitioned so hard for the installation of such technological advancements; the experience of total immersion in soothing warmth felt well worth it. Already the tightly-wound muscles in his back began to relax. He sighed in relief, letting his eyes fall shut and leaning his head back against the rim of the tub.

The faint rustle of cloth echoed off the marble walls. Aubrey opened one eye to find Lindsey disrobing as well. Already down to his drawers, he had one foot up on a convenient pillar as he removed his garters and stockings, putting his shapely leg on full display, as well as the lean muscles of his back and shoulders in bending forward.

Lindsey caught Aubrey's eye with a raised brow.

"Just enjoying the view," Aubrey assured him.

Lindsey laughed and slid his drawers off his hips with perhaps a bit more ceremony than strictly necessary. Aubrey let his eyes rove over the trim athletic form now on full display. Would that Lindsey were closer, so Aubrey might run his hands over him, as well.

As if in answer to his unspoken wish, Lindsey stepped into the bath.

Water sloshed up to the rim. Commodious as the bath was, fitting two grown men in its confines required they touch knees, at the very least. Lindsey had no qualms about coming closer still, much to Aubrey's delight.

Lindsey slid between Aubrey's thighs to wrap his long arms around his sore shoulders and deliver a slow, seductive kiss to his lips. Aubrey let himself melt into it. He willingly surrendered to Lindsey's further ministrations, as Lindsey broke off the kiss to lather up a sponge and tenderly scrub the hard-won sweat from Aubrey's skin. The whole world felt warm and soft, and by the time the last of the soap had been rinsed from both men, Aubrey's relaxation matched his exhaustion to make him thoroughly drowsy. He felt more rag-doll than man as Lindsey helped him out of the tub, towelled him off, wrapped him in a dressing gown, and led him back into the bedroom.

It took a strong force of will for Aubrey to not fall face-first onto the bed. He made a more careful and dignified descent instead, his movements halting thanks to the slow return of his aches in the absence of the warm bath, though he ended up in much the same position, lying prone atop the mattress. He felt Lindsey's weight sink into it soon after.

"Better?" Lindsey asked, laying a hand on his shoulder.

Aubrey made a noncommittal noise. Lindsey's hand began rubbing a slow figure-eight around his shoulder blades. Aubrey's muscles, made more pliant by the warm waters, greatly appreciated the attention.

"Lower," Aubrey mumbled into the pillow.

He half-expected to go unheard, yet Lindsey obliged him, clever fingers diving further down his loins to knead the knots in his lower back.

Something in Aubrey's spine cracked. He groaned in relief.

Lindsey immediately stopped his hands. "All right, there?"

"Better if you kept at it," Aubrey assured him.

Lindsey did so, working wonders upon Aubrey's flesh—and taking the opportunity to caress still lower.

Aubrey turned his head against the pillow just far enough to glimpse Lindsey over his shoulder. "Cheeky."

Lindsey bit back a cheekier grin to apologise with a kiss. "Turn over, and I'll see to the rest of you."

Aubrey obliged him.

Using the Vaseline for its intended purpose, for once, Lindsey smoothed the viscous grease over Aubrey's chafed thighs. The touch of his soft fingertips did as much as the balm itself to soothe his wounds. They did still more, as Aubrey's prick returned to the half-hard state it'd assumed in the bath.

Lindsey flashed a conspiratorial look up into Aubrey's eyes, then let his slick hands roam further north, tracing the line from Aubrey's thighs up to his hipbones. Tantalising. Aubrey's hips bucked instinctively, seeking more direct contact. Lindsey obliged him by wrapping one hand around his cock, the long fingers curling around him, applying a soft and teasing pressure before resolving into a good hard jerk.

Aubrey groaned and bucked up into his grip again. His eyes fell shut, all his senses concentrated upon Lindsey's swift, sure strokes.

Lindsey gave a breathless laugh. Then the mattress shifted underneath them, and Aubrey felt Lindsey's weight settle onto his hips, straddling him, their stiff pricks aligning as Lindsey adjusted his grip to accommodate them both. He rolled his hips in tandem with Aubrey, riding him as easily as he'd ridden his steed in the paddock, rising and falling with assured grace.

Aubrey opened his eyes just long enough to shoot a pleading look up at Lindsey, who answered it in an instant by swooping down to kiss him, to press against him and trap their cocks between their bellies, leaving only the slide of slick skin upon skin to bring them both to climax. Aubrey grabbed his arse in both hands to pull him in closer, harder, faster. He kissed Lindsey with furious passion, devouring him, fucking his mouth as much as his cock, and had the satisfaction of feeling Lindsey's astonished gasp echo in his own throat. Lindsey's cock pulsed against him, adding his seed to the slick mess between them, and the sensation sent Aubrey spilling soon after in a full-bodied shudder.

The heady combination of exhaustion and bliss meant Aubrey

didn't notice much around him for many moments. When he regained his awareness, he found his head nestled into Lindsey's collar, and Lindsey beside him with his long arms around him.

"So much for getting clean," Aubrey murmured, testing to see if Lindsey was awake.

The test proved successful. Lindsey softly chortled into Aubrey's hair, a laugh more breath than voice. "How d'you like riding so far?"

In the comfort and safety of their shared bed, Aubrey felt bold enough to admit, "I'm afraid I'm not much good at it."

"Of course not."

Aubrey couldn't help raising an eyebrow at that.

Lindsey coughed. "That is to say—I mean, you've only just begun. And nobody's any good at anything when they're starting out. So of course you're not posting the trot or jumping hedges or playing polo. Nobody is. Not when they're new at it."

"Most people begin as children," Aubrey pointed out.

"Because they have the opportunity to," Lindsey insisted. "You didn't then. But you have it now. And I think it's rather silly to come down on yourself for not mastering something new on your first day out, just because other people were fortunate enough to learn it when they were young."

Aubrey conceded the point. Lindsey happily returned to his gentle caresses—stroking Aubrey's hair, tracing his cheek, kissing his temple—equal parts tender and casual. Thus soothed, Aubrey fell to musing. He recalled Lindsey's ease upon horseback, and the dashing figure he'd cut as he posted the trot. Such a handsome vision owed as much to Lindsey's suit as it did to his skill. Riding clothes seemed designed not only to give comfort to the rider but also to flatter the rider's figure. That trim waist, those supple thighs, the polished gleam of the high leather boots…

Realisation dawned, and Aubrey lifted his head from Lindsey's collarbone to look him straight in the eyes.

"Is it possible," Aubrey asked, "that you merely wish to see me in riding costume for your own satisfaction?"

A charming blush bloomed in Lindsey's sharp cheeks. Aubrey raised his eyebrows. Lindsey coughed.

"Humour me?" he asked with a sheepish smile.

Aubrey grinned back at him. "I just might."

~

The next morning, Aubrey's chafed thighs weren't quite recovered enough for a second riding lesson, so he resigned himself to a full day of modelling.

"Can't say I'm disappointed," Halloway said when informed of the plan over breakfast. "Though I suppose you must be."

To his own surprise, Aubrey was. He wanted to capitalise on his newly-acquired horse sense while it remained fresh in his memory. But his own joints strongly disagreed with this notion. As did Lindsey.

"A day's rest won't do you any harm," Lindsey assured him. "Might do you a great deal of good, in fact."

Lindsey, meanwhile, felt perfectly able to continue riding, and, moreover, eager to get back to it. Aubrey sent him down to the stables alone and followed Halloway to his makeshift studio.

Through a combination of yesterday's sketches and referencing the chalk marks upon the tarps, Halloway guided Aubrey into the appropriate pose. Aubrey felt fortunate that the position didn't aggravate his chafed thighs, though the angle of his hips produced a twinge he hadn't noticed yesterday.

Halloway, meanwhile, returned to his easel. Rather than begin upon a canvas, he instead brought out yet another sketchbook and started whipping up watercolours.

"To test the colour palette," he explained in response to Aubrey's unasked question.

Aubrey supposed if he gained nothing else from this exercise, he would have a better understanding of the mechanics behind art. Still, he doubted even Graves would feel satisfied with hours upon hours spent lounging around as a dead mythological figure.

The distant chiming of the grandfather clock in the foyer marked the passing of another hour. Halloway, apparently satisfied with his watercolour sketches at last, set them aside. From behind the makeshift background, Halloway pulled out an enormous canvas which Aubrey felt quite certain hadn't been there yesterday.

"Stretched and *gesso*'d it last afternoon," Halloway said in response to Aubrey's bewildered look. As Aubrey's confusion didn't immediately dissipate, he then went on to further explain how he'd transported the rolled-up canvas and disassembled frame—four wooden slats that Aubrey had disregarded before as spare bits of easel. Then, whilst Aubrey had his horseback-riding misadventures, Halloway had hammered the frame together, unrolled the canvas, stretched it tight over the frame, nailed it into place, and slathered the whole surface in a preliminary coat of primer, *alias gesso*.

"Now that's it's dry," Halloway concluded, "we can move on to the final stages."

Through sharing a lodging house with Halloway, Aubrey had grown familiar with the distinctive chemical smell of the oil painting process. The smell of Halloway's studio didn't permeate the whole house, thank God, but it did waft out into the hallway, and whenever Aubrey had passed by the door on his way down from his garret out into the street, he'd caught a whiff of it, sharp and strong.

Even so, upon watching Halloway prepare his palette, Aubrey discovered some of his assumptions had proved false. It was not the paints themselves that smelled—it was the thinner.

Halloway, explaining the chemistry behind the art as he squeezed dollops of paint from their tubes, told him how the pigment was suspended in plant-based carrier oils such as linseed or walnut. These, as Aubrey could detect in that very moment with his own nose, had little smell—though Halloway admitted cadmium red had a heavy metallic tang.

The paint thinner, however, smelled quite strong. And as Aubrey watched Halloway pour it out into a jar, he realised he'd spent years wrinkling his nose at common turpentine.

"You get used to it," Halloway said in his typical off-handed way.

Aubrey wondered if Halloway could still smell the stuff, and if not, whether Halloway could smell much of anything at all anymore.

However, the Wiltshire house ballroom was a far cry from Halloway's rooms in the Manchester lodging house. The sheer enormity of the space allowed the fumes to disperse almost as well as if Halloway had chosen to paint *en plein air*. Even just cracking open a few of the French windows did wonders for ventilation.

Aubrey quickly forgot the scent of turpentine as Halloway swirled the blunted palette knife through the dollops of paint, blending the base colours to create new and brilliant hues. The process proved transfixing beyond Aubrey's expectations. Oil and pigment swirled in a dizzying array. Halloway's brush flitted between the palette and the canvas, laying down swathes of colour which, before Aubrey's eyes, transformed into a blurred yet recognisable representation of the rocky seashore Icarus was supposed to have washed up upon. Almost as if viewed through a clouded lens, or a window lashed with rain. The mere impression of an image.

Then Halloway gently suggested Aubrey might return to the faux seashore so the painting could truly begin, and Aubrey settled back down upon the sheets and cushions to let Halloway get to work.

"How are you enjoying riding?" Halloway asked.

It rather amazed Aubrey how effortlessly Halloway could carry on a conversation whilst he worked. He supposed it came after years of painting portraits—a task which must prove awkward for the two parties involved if carried out in total silence. "Well enough."

Halloway chuckled, still not taking his eyes from his task. "Damned by faint praise."

Aubrey, having intended nothing of the sort, hurried to correct Halloway's impression. "I'm still trying to get my seat right in the saddle. Haven't even picked up the reins yet. But Lindsey's been very patient with me so far. And Fletcher's a fine teacher."

"Fletcher?"

"The groom."

Halloway made an affirmative sound. Silence grew in its wake. With nothing to distract himself, Aubrey's mind continued alone down the increasingly treacherous path of their conversation.

"Not a bad way to spend a holiday," Halloway observed as if their conversation had never lapsed.

"I suppose," Aubrey replied without thinking. Then his thinking caught up to his tongue, and he found himself confessing, "I'm afraid I'm rather useless."

Halloway's brush stopped daubing the canvas. "How so?"

"Converting the Rook Mill to electricity has to wait until Emmeline returns. Likewise installing electric lights in the Manchester house and the London house and here. So I can't do any productive engineering, but instead of looking for other work, I'm either lying on cushions or falling off a horse."

Halloway gave him a considering look. "Have you ever taken a holiday before?"

Giving a straightforward answer felt too much like admitting defeat for Aubrey's taste. "I don't like not working."

"With all due respect," Halloway replied gravely, "you are

working."

Aubrey furrowed his brow in confusion. "Beg pardon?"

"You're modelling." Halloway shrugged. "It might not be hard labour, but it is labour. It requires skill—the ability to follow instruction and to maintain a pose, both of which are harder than you might think, and dashed difficult to find in a muse—and it earns a wage."

"No it doesn't," Aubrey replied without thinking.

Halloway raised his eyebrows at him. "It most certainly does. At least in my studio. And in that of any other respectable painter."

"But you're not paying me," Aubrey protested.

Halloway balked. "I most certainly am!"

Aubrey stared at him.

Halloway continued. "Very first day we met, I offered you compensation for modelling. At the time, you declined. More recently, you accepted. Same offer. Same wage." Halloway hesitated. "At least, that's how I understood it. How did you?"

"Thought I was just doing a favour for a friend." It sounded stupid, once admitted aloud.

Halloway, too, appeared abashed. "Oh. That's—very kind of you." A shy smile twitched at his moustache. "Very kind indeed. I'll not press the wage on you if you don't want it, but… I really do prefer to pay my models."

"What about your portrait subjects?"

"They pay me because they keep the painting. And because they come to me to paint it in the first place. I didn't paint Mrs Bellingham because I thought she had cheekbones worthy of Olympus. I painted her because her husband wanted her likeness preserved for the ages by the hand of master." Halloway twirled his paintbrush in his fingers. "If it's not too bold of me to say."

"Oh." It occurred to Aubrey just who Halloway thought might have cheekbones worthy of Olympus. Those same cheeks blushed all the harder for it.

"I suppose you can keep the painting in lieu of wages, if you'd prefer," Halloway conceded. "Though I'd really hoped to exhibit it. Show off my talents, drum up business, that sort of thing. Make a bit of a ripple in the greater artistic pool, if I'm lucky. Sell it off to someone who shares my appreciation for Classical legend and the male form—though hopefully with deeper pockets."

Until now, Aubrey hadn't given much thought to what would become of the painting once Halloway finished it. He'd assumed it might go into a portrait hall not unlike the one full of Lindsey's ancestors in this very house, rarely exhibited, and only privately examined. Halloway's revelation—that he'd intended the work for public exhibition and sale—rather threw a wrench into Aubrey's assumptions.

But rather than admit his own misapprehensions, Aubrey asked, "You've exhibited other paintings previously?"

"Indeed I have—Contrary to popular belief, it would seem!" Halloway replied in good humour. "They do tolerably well. Garner some reviews in more out-of-the-way publications. And they sell, which is a rarer thing for art than you might think. But more importantly, the interest they generate encourages new portrait clients, which is the real bread-and-butter of the business. And," he added with a mischievous twitch of his moustache, "I rather enjoy painting them."

"Are they usually of Classical scenes?"

Halloway furrowed his brow as he considered the question, his brush flitting between canvas and palette all the while. "You know, I've never quite broken it down mathematically. But if I had to estimate, I'd say about half of them are Classical, a third medieval, and whatever's left a sort of vulgar hodge-podge."

Aubrey, who'd spent the last few minutes trying to find a delicate phrasing for his most pressing inquiry, gave up. "Are they all nude?"

The question which so strained Aubrey's personal sense of propriety didn't appear to give Halloway anywhere near so much strife. "Certainly not the medieval ones. Absolutely smothered in velvet, they are. But one can get away with a great deal more when it comes to the Classical. I suspect that's a great part of why they're so popular."

The thought of such popularity made Aubrey feel somewhat queasy. He'd been popular once before, as a telegraph boy, amongst men who greatly desired his naked form. Returning to such a state after having worked so hard to escape it didn't sit well with him. Furthermore, whilst he'd been called strikingly beautiful as a youth, he knew his appearance hadn't been so distinctive as to remain recognisable long after he'd grown out of the trade.

But now, in the wake of the boiler explosion at Rook Mill, his steam burns had left him with a face that shocked passers-by into open-mouthed horror. Such a face would burn into the memories of all who saw *Icarus Fallen*. He couldn't hope for anything like anonymity with the new and far more distinctive likeness he wore now. Not only his face, but his naked body would once again be on display, with the same unmistakable scars running all along it.

"Or," said Halloway, interrupting Aubrey's thoughts once more, "I could keep it for myself. Vain and selfish though it may mark me, I think this may become one of my better pieces, and I'd be happy to admire it in my own rooms for many years."

Yet Halloway wasn't admiring the painting now. He was looking straight into Aubrey's eyes, and the casual cast of his expression appeared more forced than before.

Aubrey knew at once Halloway had made the offer only in response to Aubrey's evident discomfort. Whilst Aubrey appreciated the gesture, as a friend, he could not allow himself to accept such a bargain. Halloway shouldn't be forced to compromise his career for the sake of Aubrey's weakness of character. His fears were unfounded, borne of vanity, of assuming anyone could bear to gaze upon such hideous features long enough to recognise them.

Besides, Aubrey thought, with more than a hint of wicked satisfaction, wouldn't it give his old admirers a shock to see what had become of their Ganymede.

~

Luncheon consisted of sirloin steak with fried tomatoes, lamb chops with spinach, and fresh strawberries with cream. Meat so tender it fell apart under the knife, tomatoes fried to a satisfying crisp, sweet strawberries with cream fresh from the dairy, any one of these far better fare than Aubrey had known before he'd met Lindsey.

"Keep the kitchen maid," Halloway advised between bites, and Aubrey had to agree.

After luncheon, Lindsey went out riding, while Halloway attempted to teach Aubrey to play billiards. It went better than any attempt made in Aubrey's youth at the Catullus Club, probably because Halloway actually wanted Aubrey to learn the rules and strategies of the game, and not just stare at his arse as he bent over the table. The billiards room at the Wiltshire house also possessed the advantage of a splendid view outside of its windows, one which just so happened to overlook the stables, and allowed Aubrey to catch sight of Lindsey's return some hours later.

"He does cut a rather dashing figure," Halloway mused.

Aubrey, watching Lindsey race across the fields like Dick Turpin on Black Bess, again found himself agreeing with Halloway's assessment.

"You can go on ahead," Halloway continued, returning to the business of chalking a cue. "I'll finish up here."

Aubrey hadn't said anything aloud about his desire to go down and meet Lindsey upon his return but supposed something in his expression had told the astute painter all his intentions. Regardless, he took advantage of the offer and went out.

The long and winding path on foot from the billiards room to the courtyard brought Aubrey to the stables just as Lindsey rode into the paddock on horseback.

Lindsey, despite the distraction of riding, locked eyes with Aubrey the moment he arrived. His already-brilliant smile brightened further, and he leapt down from the saddle with the grace of a dancer. Handing the reins off to a groom, he began striding towards Aubrey.

But the coachman—recognisable as such by his age, some twenty years older than the grooms, and by the deference they showed him—stepped into Lindsey's path.

"If you'll forgive the interruption, sir," he said with a brief touch of his hat-brim. "I've heard tell of a fine piece of horseflesh for sale."

This offer appeared to greatly intrigue Lindsey. Before he could continue his discussion with the coachman, however, he turned to address Aubrey.

"Go on ahead to the house," said Lindsey. "I'll be along shortly."

Aubrey, abashed by how easily Lindsey had seen through his efforts to disguise his bewildered boredom, nevertheless felt relieved at his release, and slipped out of the stable as the coachman continued describing the prospective addition to the herd.

The path between the stables and the house split at the paddock, the right-hand path going straight on to meet the gravel of the courtyard and the massive granite steps up into the house, and the left-hand path taking a more circuitous route behind the stable and on through the gardens. Aubrey, assuming Lindsey's discussion with the coachman would last some minutes, took the left-hand path to while away the time amongst pleasant scenery.

Yet before he ever reached the pleasant scenery, while still approaching the rear of the stables, the sound of conversation drifted to his ears.

"And of course," a man's voice drawled in the tone of one who believed himself an under-appreciated wit, "he looked a right beauty when last he came."

The familiar burning blush crept up the nape of Aubrey's neck. He paused on the pathway, uncertain. A wise man would turn back. No benefit could derive from idle gossip.

Yet Aubrey knew himself more curious than wise, and so he continued on the path which by purest coincidence brought him nearer to the voice.

"But now," the voice continued as Aubrey walked, "I shudder to think what'd happen if he should chance to stroll past the dairy. That face would sour milk in the udder."

If Aubrey had harboured any hopes that he was not the subject of conversation, these hopes sank now. Amongst the uniformly handsome staff, and the dashing good looks of Lindsey, the only man in the house whose face could be said to sour milk belonged to Aubrey himself.

With a knot in his stomach to match the burning in his ears, Aubrey reached the back of the stable and peered around the corner to see who spoke thus.

The stable boy—more man than boy, really, standing just as tall as the grooms and twice as broad—scrubbed down a horse with a handful of dry straw, whilst a footman leaned against a post to watch the proceedings. The footman, whom Aubrey could tell apart from the grooms only by virtue of his livery, appeared far more interested in the stable boy's rippling muscles than in the horse. Aubrey couldn't blame him. Yet the stable hand, intent on his work, appeared to take no notice of the footman in turn.

"It's a wonder Sir Lindsey can bear to look upon it," said the footman, revealing himself as the disembodied voice. "Though I suppose there's no accounting for taste."

Aubrey, who'd wondered the same thing often enough in his darker moments, nonetheless felt sick at the confirmation that others thought so.

"Perhaps we ought to put a bell on him," the footman continued, "so we might know when he's coming and prepare ourselves for the sight."

"At least he's not ugly on the inside, which is more'n I can say for the likes of you."

The addition of a second voice shocked the footman as much as it did Aubrey. The stable hand spoke low and level, nothing like the lilting performance of the footman.

"What're you on about?" the footman demanded, all decorum vanished.

"I'm sayin' your soul turns stomachs," said the stable hand, never raising his eyes from his task. "Mine included."

The footman stared in frank disbelief at the stable hand. The stable hand continued working in silence. After a moment, the footman gave a loud scoff, turned on his heel and strode out of the stable yard, taking the path behind it up to the house.

Aubrey, disinclined to immediately follow in the footsteps of one who held him in such disdain, turned back down the path—as he ought to have done when he first stumbled upon a private conversation, he reflected in bitter self-reproach—and came to the front of the stables just as Lindsey re-emerged, ebullient as ever.

"Connor has espied a fine yearling," Lindsey told him by way of explanation. "Magnificent blue roan coat, a colouring to which Rowena is quite partial. I'm inclined to wait until she returns to have her opinion on the matter, though some other more decisive fellow may have snatched it up by then. What d'you think?"

Aubrey forced a smile and confessed he had no thoughts upon it whatsoever.

Dinner that evening may as well have been so much ash for all Aubrey could taste it. Likewise, he heard little of the conversation between Lindsey and Halloway regarding the potential new horse.

After dinner, Halloway retired early, intending to rise before dawn so he might make himself ready to paint in the morning's light. This left Aubrey and Lindsey alone together in the library. Aubrey had assumed they might pass the hours in silent reading of the evening papers and those magazines which had only just been forwarded from the London townhouse. These hopes were dashed as Lindsey set aside the most recent issue of *Belgravia* and turned to address him directly.

"Have you any opinion on the new cook?" Lindsey asked.

Aubrey, who could barely remember having eaten, could only respond with a blank look.

"You hardly touched the asparagus vinaigrette," Lindsey noted. "I thought the Welsh rabbit might prove more to your liking, but..."

"I'm afraid I hadn't much appetite," Aubrey admitted.

"Not ill, I hope," said Lindsey, and seemed ready to leave his chair to put a hand upon Aubrey's forehead.

Aubrey, his guilt compounding, hurried to reply. "I'm fine. Just distracted."

Lindsey eased back into his seat with an expression of fond relief. "Engineering, I suppose?"

As much as Aubrey wanted to take the easy out Lindsey had offered him, he felt guilty enough as matters stood without lying outright. He shook his head, chewed his tongue, and at length, forced out, "You were saying something about selecting staff for the Manchester house?"

"Indeed!" said Lindsey, obviously delighted to have Aubrey's opinion on the matter at last. "Have you any preference?"

"Do they have to come from here?"

Lindsey fixed him with a befuddled expression. "No, I don't suppose they must. Though it would certainly expedite the process. Rowena has already chosen those least inclined to taking offence to our living arrangements."

Aubrey supposed that was as good a euphemism as any for it. "And least inclined towards blackmail."

Lindsey sobered. "One must hope so."

And yet, Aubrey knew, not the least inclined towards gossip. "How does she confirm their character?"

"Through a lengthy interview process before and good wages after. At least, that's what I've always assumed." A crease appeared between Lindsey's brows. "What's troubling you?"

"Nothing," Aubrey lied.

It evidently did not convince Lindsey, who set aside his magazine, hesitated, then said at last, "If you insist. Though if there is anything amiss, I wish you'd tell me."

Aubrey weighed his complaint against the gravity of its consequences. He didn't want anyone to lose their place over it. It wasn't their fault he looked as he did. Still, if they couldn't stand the sight of him, he didn't particularly want to live with them in such close quarters as the Manchester house provided.

Though, as he reflected upon it, he knew some members of the household staff who didn't think him unforgivably ugly.

"You said we require a housemaid as well as a cook?" Aubrey asked.

Lindsey nodded.

"I think," Aubrey went on in halting fashion, "I may have someone to nominate for that post."

Surprise elevated Lindsey's eyebrows. "Splendid! Who?"

This simple question quite overran Aubrey's power to answer. "A dark-haired girl. Welsh, I think. I'm afraid I don't know her name. But she seems well-suited to the work and might do well for us in Manchester."

"That's certainly more opinion than I've been able to form on the subject." Lindsey furrowed his brow in thought. "It's a shame you can't name her, but I'm sure Mrs Sheffield will know her from description."

"Good," said Aubrey.

He'd hoped that would be the end of the matter, yet Lindsey continued gazing upon him with an expression of concern. Aubrey cast his own eyes down to the latest issue of *The Engineer*, pretending to read a few sentences before glancing up at Lindsey again from under his lashes—only to find Lindsey's attention had not waned.

"Forgive me for prying," said Lindsey with the hapless smile of one caught out. "Only I can't shake the notion there's something else."

"It's my own fault for eavesdropping," Aubrey muttered.

Lindsey, of course, caught every word. "Eavesdropping on whom? What have you heard?"

Aubrey attempted a casual shrug, as he'd seen Graves and Halloway perform time and again. "Nothing. Just some of the staff talking."

"What about?" asked Lindsey, undeterred.

Aubrey, out of subterfuge and exhausted with attempting it, gave in. "My face."

For some moments, the crackling of the fire in the hearth provided the only sound.

"Who," Lindsey said at last, in a tone Aubrey hadn't heard from him in quite some time.

"I don't know!" Aubrey protested. "A footman. I don't know his name."

"What did he say?"

"Nothing worth sacking him over."

Lindsey, his mouth already open to retort and his expression hardened in anger, froze. At length he shut his mouth, swallowed hard, and in gentler tones, replied, "If you insist. Though I think a stern correction is due, at the very least."

"It doesn't matter," Aubrey insisted.

"You matter."

The assertion, simple as it sounded, gave Aubrey more cause for astonishment than he cared to admit. All the more so for the firm tone with which it was said. Lindsey did not often have cause to speak in a commanding fashion. Nor did his face often appear without at least a hint of good humour dancing in his eyes. Yet here Lindsey sat, determination carved into every feature of his handsome visage, as he stared into Aubrey's face with an intensity as arousing as it was unnerving. Passion burned in his gaze. And to be the subject of such a passion… well. Aubrey could appreciate that much, at least, even if he felt it misplaced.

Unable to manage any coherent reply around the growing lump in his throat, Aubrey instead rose from his own chair and bent to kiss his valiant Lindsey.

The passion which had sparked in Lindsey's eyes proved just as strong in his lips, and for some moments no conversation could pass between them, for they had not breath to spare.

~

"I'd say you're about ready to take the reins, sir. If you'd be willin' to give it a go."

Aubrey, stunned, blinked down at Fletcher from his perch in the saddle atop Parsival. The groom had offered his comment unprompted, after yet another turn around the paddock identical to every other turn before it. Perhaps the monotony itself had prompted him; Aubrey's ability to retain his seat turn after turn having proved him reliable enough to take charge of the matter.

"I'm willing," Aubrey replied.

With an adept flick of his wrist, Fletcher brought the reins up over

Parsival's head and held them out for Aubrey to take.

The leather strap, slender as it was, nevertheless seemed to weigh a great deal in Aubrey's fingers. He closed both fists tight around it.

"You may find, sir," said Fletcher, "that a softer touch might serve you better."

Aubrey, duly chastened, went against every instinct and relaxed his grip on the reins. Parsival flicked his ears to rid himself of a fly and otherwise took no notice.

"See here, sir," Fletcher explained, patting the gelding's cheek to induce him to turn his head into Aubrey's view. "This—" Fletcher pointed to the metal part of the bridle in Parsival's mouth. "—is the bit. Your touch on the reins presses it against his gums, which tells him to turn to one side or the other, or to halt outright. You needn't pull very hard; he's clever enough to know what's wanted of him."

Aubrey nodded his understanding.

Fletcher continued, leaving go of Parsival's head to approach Aubrey in the saddle. He raised his hands to indicate Aubrey's arm without touching it. "When you do put pressure on the reins, you might feel tempted to pull up. I would encourage you instead to pull back—gentle-like—and keep your forearms level with the ground. In most cases, you needn't do much more than turn your wrist. Here." He held up a closed fist, then turned his hand over into a more relaxed position. "Let the reins lay in your palm, and your fingers fold over it."

Aubrey did as he was told.

"Just so, sir," said Fletcher. "If you're ready, then, you c'n try urgin' him on with your knees. His head and neck move as he walks—he can't help that—and you'll just keep the reins steady in your hand until you need him to turn. Don't let it tighten up when he puts his head out, or slacken when he pulls his neck in. Try to keep a consistent feel of his mouth. You'll see what I mean in a moment. Keep your arms loose and your hands ready, and you'll do all right."

Taking control of such a massive animal felt like rather more responsibility than Aubrey had ever assumed in his life, but he nodded to Fletcher again regardless of the growing knot in his stomach.

Fletcher stepped back. "There you go, sir."

With great trepidation, Aubrey gently pressed his knees against the gelding's sides. It seemed foolish to suppose his limbs could make any impression upon the huge beast's flesh, its muscles shifting under his seat and thighs, each breath like a tide rising and falling beneath him.

And yet, true to Fletcher's word, Parsival stepped forward.

In an instant, Aubrey realised what Fletcher meant about tightening and slackening the reins. With every step, Parsival's head bobbed up and down—as it had done every turn 'round the paddock before now, Aubrey supposed, only with all his attention upon keeping his seat, he'd never taken much notice. Now, he alternately grasped and released the reins to keep a consistent tension.

"Just so, sir," Fletcher said again, his voice coming from behind Aubrey now that he and Parsival had left the groom behind. "Tight on the left..."

Aubrey pulled his left hand back—not up—until he felt a resistance.

And then that resistance gave way as Parsival's head turned to the left, and the rest of the gelding followed, bringing them both around the edge of the paddock.

"Nicely done, sir," said Fletcher.

Aubrey, still not quite believing he had any control over the beast, didn't dare look over his shoulder to acknowledge the groom's praise. Yet a victorious smile stole over his face nonetheless.

Parsival continued walking along the paddock's perimeter until they came to the part of the fence where Lindsey stood, his forearms on the uppermost bar, leaning forward in eagerness with a winning smile to match Aubrey's own.

A few widdershins turns around the paddock later, and a few more clockwise after that, Aubrey dismounted from Parsival, without much grace, but unassisted.

"How do you like the reins, then?" Lindsey asked him as Fletcher took the gelding back into the stable.

"Well enough," said Aubrey. Satisfied for the moment that none of the grooms stood within earshot, he confessed in a lower tone, "Rather a lot of responsibility."

"Heavy is the head who wears the crown," Lindsey offered up with an air of quotation. "It must follow, then, that heavy is the hand which holds the reins."

Aubrey bit back a laugh and followed him back up to the house.

Whilst Aubrey went upstairs to exchange his suit for one which smelled less of horses, Lindsey continued on ahead of him to the library. Aubrey knew the route between it and the master bedroom better than any other. As such, when it came time for him to rejoin Lindsey, he felt more confident than otherwise in taking a right-hand turn in place of a left and bringing himself down by another path in an effort to better familiarise himself with the house. His wanderings brought him past the billiards room—unexpected, yet not unwelcome. Beyond the billiards room he found a parlour, its furniture covered in white sheets in defence against dust. He concluded this must be a room more often used by Rowena and abandoned in her absence.

Past the parlour the corridor split in twain, and as Aubrey turned left, he crossed paths with a maid emerging from one of the rooms. As she shut the door behind herself, she bent her head, and so he spotted her before she realised his presence. In doing so, he recognised her as the maid he'd overheard the other day—the one who agreed to replace the one who feared his face.

By the time she looked up, Aubrey had regained some control over his alarmed expression and continued down the corridor. He nodded as he passed her. She bowed her head and gave a quick curtsy. By the bounds of etiquette, that should have been the end of the matter.

And yet, as Aubrey walked on, he found something in him gnawing for more. Perhaps the success of taking the reins had emboldened him, for he stopped, turned, and said, "I beg your pardon, miss."

The maid's initial surprise at being thus addressed quickly gave way to wariness, and with hesitance, she replied, "Yes, sir?"

Aubrey could hardly blame her for her suspicion. He knew better than most that gentlemen typically only noticed their so-called lessers for one reason. And he could hardly assure her he had no interest in her for that particular purpose without making their conversation even more awkward. Still, he had a pressing question to ask. "What is your name?"

"Owen, sir. Winifred."

"Thank you, Miss Owen."

The startled flash in her dark eyes told him he'd erred. It took him a moment to realise how. Aubrey, used to considering the servant class upon an equal footing with himself, had addressed her as he might any woman working in the mills: by assumed title and surname. Whereas, of course, most gentleman addressed their staff by their Christian names, if at all.

Before she could say anything in response, Aubrey gave her a brisk nod and scampered away from the site of his latest shame as fast as his waning dignity would allow.

~

By the end of Tuesday's riding lesson, Fletcher deemed Aubrey a fair enough rider to go beyond the paddock and out into the wider countryside with Lindsey.

Lindsey felt no small measure of pride at his clever Aubrey's quick progress. He suffused most of it into a hearty clap of Aubrey's shoulder. While he knew he had nothing to fear from showing his particular affections in front of his staff, he still had a natural hesitance of flaunting his intimacy in their presence—to say nothing of Aubrey's discomfort. Such considerations only made Lindsey all the more eager to ride out with Aubrey. To enjoy the fresh air of the countryside whilst rejoicing in the affection of his beloved, in the peculiar anonymity of the wilderness… Lindsey craved it more than words could say.

Wednesday dawned as bright as every day previous. The sun shone no less bright in the early afternoon than it had in the morning. The only clouds appeared gleaming white and fluffy, friendly and gossamer, nothing like the heavy green-grey smog that hung over Manchester.

For his own mount, Lindsey selected Atalanta, the only mare in the stable not belonging to his sister. Aubrey went on the gelding Parsival, as he had for all his riding lessons.

The ride began much like the riding lessons. On this occasion Aubrey mounted his steed unassisted, with determined strength if not ease or grace. Lindsey felt a mixture of admiration and wistfulness as he watched. Though he would never dare wound Aubrey's pride by mentioning it, he had rather enjoyed helping Aubrey up. Still, there was something to be said for the sight of a handsome man springing into the saddle—particularly when, once seated, said handsome man turned to flash a smile of secret triumph at Lindsey.

As they rode side-by-side out of the stable yard, Lindsey kept his eyes on Aubrey as much or more than on the path ahead. Aubrey started the ride with his jaw clenched and brow furrowed, but as they continued on their journey, he gradually relaxed, until he reached a point of comfort where he evidently felt safe enough to take his eyes off his steed's ears and catch Lindsey's look. Surprise flitted over Aubrey's features, then another smile, broader and longer-lasting than the one in the stable yard, now that it had no audience save Lindsey. Lindsey responded in kind, his heart warmed by the knowledge that such a smile was meant for him and him alone.

At length, Aubrey grew comfortable enough in the saddle to converse. He told Lindsey all about the morning's modelling and how the painting progressed. Lindsey confessed himself eager to see the finished product.

Aubrey hesitated, then said, "You could see it now. I don't think Halloway would mind."

Lindsey gave him a considering look. He knew well the expression on Aubrey's face—the worrying of the lower lip between his teeth. "Would *you* mind?"

The question came in the gentlest tone Lindsey possessed, yet no listener could deny its pointed nature.

Aubrey glanced away for a moment, his brow furrowed.

"It's all right if you do," said Lindsey.

An appreciative smile flickered across Aubrey's lips. "I don't mind. It's just... odd. I've never modelled before. Much to Halloway's frustration."

"He's not short with you, is he?" Halloway didn't seem the type, but if he proved himself a cad, Lindsey wouldn't hesitate to come to Aubrey's defence.

"Oh no, nothing of the sort," Aubrey replied easily. "He's a perfect gentleman about the business. Only I think he wishes I'd taken him up on his offer earlier." His expression turned wistful, and he cocked his head in such a way as to bring his burn scars into the sun.

Lindsey knew, of course, that Halloway had chosen the subject of Icarus specifically to take full advantage of Aubrey's distinctive appearance, but he didn't think it would help to remind Aubrey of that now. Nor would it help to reassure Aubrey that he remained devastatingly handsome. So instead, Lindsey replied, "He's lucky to have you model for him at all, no matter when."

Aubrey's eyes widened, and for an instant Lindsey feared he'd made the issue worse, until a bark of laughter burst from Aubrey's throat.

Parsival snorted, and Atalanta's ears swivelled, but Lindsey's calm suffused his horse and her partner in turn, despite the sudden sound. His own laughter reverberated through his chest, and he pressed his lips firmly together to contain it, until he felt certain he would let out no more than a quiet chuckle.

Aubrey, meanwhile, had clapped a hand over his mouth to prevent further outbursts whilst he recovered himself. When he dropped his hand at last, he had an easy grin to match Lindsey's own.

"Have you ever had your portrait painted?" Aubrey asked.

"I haven't," Lindsey replied. "The family tradition is to wait until the subject has come into his own, as it were—inherited a title, or married."

"You've already done the one," Aubrey pointed out. "And you're less than a year away from the other."

"True enough, though I had always assumed such events would occur in the reverse order."

Lindsey had only thought aloud as he spoke, though the reminder of his father's passing gave him pause, and judging from the knitting of Aubrey's brow, the same occurred to him. Aubrey moved his arm as if to lay a hand on Lindsey's shoulder, then hesitated, doubtless rethinking the instinctive gesture in light of both men sitting astride horses at that moment. Still, Lindsey appreciated the effort and hoped his thankful smile said as much.

"Are you suggesting," Lindsey continued, "that you suppose I am overdue to sit for a portrait?"

"Not in so many words," said Aubrey. He stopped himself again, and when he resumed speaking, he did so with a bashful air. "I just think your face is worth preserving, is all."

Lindsey couldn't help teasing him. "As a curiosity, no doubt."

"As a work of art!" Aubrey protested.

Lindsey raised his brows.

Realisation dawned over Aubrey's face, and his cheeks turned a delightful rosy shade. "You're a damned handsome gent, and you know it as well as I."

Lindsey shrugged, unable to stop himself from smiling at the compliment. "If you insist."

"I do," said Aubrey.

His firm tone surprised Lindsey, who turned his gaze from the road ahead to see Aubrey's dark brows furrowed in determination.

"I don't say it often enough," Aubrey continued—Lindsey would've protested this assertion, but Aubrey didn't give him the chance. "But you're handsome, and kind, and... a good man."

The "I love you" went unspoken, as they rode along out-of-doors where anyone might hear, but Lindsey felt it echoing in his heart as clearly as if Aubrey had shouted it.

Aubrey cleared his throat. "And I think someone ought to try their hand at preserving at least some of that."

"Halloway, you mean," said Lindsey, his fond smile turning wry at the corners.

"He's not half-bad at it," Aubrey admitted.

"True enough. How would you like to see me painted? Standing in the library? Or laid out like the *Venus of Urbino*?"

"If you mean without your clothes on, I can't say I'd mind it." Aubrey said, his smile matching Lindsey's. "Though I don't think you could hang it in the family gallery."

"Standing in the library for the gallery, then," Lindsey conceded. "And reclining nude for you."

Aubrey's cheeks had once again turned a charming shade of porcelain pink, like the inside of a seashell. "If you're offering."

"I am. Volunteering, even. With enthusiasm."

"Then as long as you are," Aubrey added, not meeting Lindsey's twinkling eyes, "perhaps you'd also sit for something smaller. And more... traditional."

"Interesting euphemism for 'put your clothes back on,'" Lindsey mused aloud. A spark of understanding put a stop to his teasing. "You mean a miniature?"

"Yes," Aubrey blurted.

Lindsey blinked at him.

Aubrey spluttered on. "It's rather foolish, I know—it's not like you're going away to sea and I need something to remember you by—but—I still—"

In truth, since the explosion at the mill, they'd rarely spent more than a few days apart. Not that either of them minded. And yet.

"You still want me?" Lindsey gently prompted, as Aubrey's speech seemed choked by the intensity of his own desires.

Relief washed over Aubrey's face. "I do."

Lindsey felt his own cheeks warming to match Aubrey's, even as a smile spread across them. "Then I'd be happy to sit for a miniature. On one condition."

Aubrey looked puzzled. "Name it."

"I'd like one of you, in turn."

This answer did nothing to un-puzzle Aubrey's expression, though an astonished smile broke through his bemusement. "If you insist."

"I do."

Aubrey bit his lower lip and looked away, bashful as ever, out across the fields to the woods beyond. Lindsey followed his gaze, admiring the gentle sway of the top-most branches, though not quite so much as he admired the sharp line of Aubrey's jaw.

The summer breeze—which 'til now had gently plucked at the ends of their horses' manes—picked up. The top-most branches of the woods swayed with greater speed and violence. Lindsey realized the leaves were not merely fluttering in the wind; they had turned over entirely, showing their lighter-coloured backs to the sky. Looking to the sky himself, Lindsey saw the fluffy white clouds had gathered together into a single grey mass, and that grey mass darkened with every passing moment, with coal-black clumps of thunderheads on its heels.

"Should we turn—" Aubrey began.

"Yes," said Lindsey.

The single syllable came sharp and cold with forced calm. Lindsey glanced back to Aubrey and found the last traces of a hastily-hidden look of surprise.

"Lead on," said Aubrey, with as much or more determination as Lindsey had expressed.

Lindsey forced a smile and turned Atalanta back upon the path they'd come. It took a few moments more for Aubrey to coax Parsival into the same direction, and by the time they started back in earnest, raindrops pelted the path. Lindsey hoped it might remain a light summer shower, but even as he did so, the raindrops redoubled, turning the dusty path to dark mud. Worse yet, a distant rumbling echoed across the skies.

If only, Lindsey mused, he had waited until Aubrey had learnt to trot before they had gone out riding. If only the weather had shown its true colours before they'd set out. If only he had noticed the change sooner and turned them back even minutes ago. As matters stood now, they'd be soaked through by the time they arrived at the stables.

More rumbling resounded across the fields. Undeniable thunder. Atalanta's ears flicked 'round. Lindsey bid her remain steady. He looked to Aubrey beside him, wondering if he ought to take Parsival's reins out of Aubrey's hands, pride be damned.

Lightning flashed.

And everything exploded.

Both horses shrieked. Atalanta leapt to the side. Lindsey kept his seat, just barely, and concentrated his efforts on turning her head so she couldn't bolt. She spun twice before she finally shook off her spook. The moment she halted, Lindsey looked up to see how Aubrey fared on Parsival.

Only to find both horse and rider had vanished.

~

CHAPTER FIVE

Lindsey stared at the road where Aubrey had ridden just moments before. He'd expected to find him struggling to regain control over his spooked steed, or laid out in the mud whilst Parsival galloped off for the hills.

But to find Aubrey simply gone, as if faeries had plucked him out of reality, was more unnerving than the worst Lindsey had imagined.

Lindsey dropped the reins, slipped his boots out of his stirrups, and swung himself out of the saddle and down. Atalanta didn't like that, on top of her spook. The moment Lindsey splashed into the mud, she bolted.

This wasn't so worrisome. She knew the way to the stables as well as any other beast and could seek shelter on her own. Better to not have to worry about keeping a frightened steed under control. He could focus on finding Aubrey.

Thunder rumbled overhead. Lindsey, wary of being the tallest thing in an open field during a storm, abandoned the road for the moment to seek shelter in the shadow of a boulder. Crouched down in the grass and muck, he reminded himself that he couldn't very well help Aubrey if he got himself struck by lightning. Running out into danger now would make him no better than the foolish horses. He had to keep his head. To think.

A difficult task, when his mind screamed at him that his Aubrey was gone, gone, gone.

Rain poured down. Lindsey watched the clouds rolling overhead, shielding his eyes from the rain with one hand. Lightning split the sky again and again, chased by deafening thunder. He tried not to think of the possibility that any of those strikes might have hit Aubrey.

He knew not how long he waited. Rain soaked him through, spilling down the collar of his coat into his shirt, sticking his breeches to his legs, and draining into his boots. His knees ached with crouching.

Then, at last, the thunder rolled away and took the lightning with it. He counted the seconds without a strike. The seconds turned into minutes. In those minutes, the rain slowed from a driving downpour to a mere steady stream. At last, he felt satisfied that the worst was over, though it yet rained, and stood up to begin his search.

The turf, soaked through with sudden rain, proved no match for Parsival's hooves. Every panicked stride had carved deep into the mud.

Lindsey wasted no time in following the trail.

The gouges in the ground led him from the road across the field—every step sucking at his boots—over a fence—a worrisome thought, that Parsival had taken a panicked leap with Aubrey upon his back, though Lindsey saw no sign that Aubrey had become unseated in that particular adventure—and across another field abutting it. Lindsey slogged through it all, his eyes fixed upon the ground before him, hunting out the next track, until the mud and grass underfoot turned to damp dead leaves, and he looked up to find himself on the edge of the woods.

Lindsey tried to take heart. By fleeing into the trees, Parsival, and by extension Aubrey, would be sheltered from the rain and lightning alike. Yet the ground, sheltered by those very same trees, did not show Parsival's passing so clearly as the muddied fields.

Now glancing up for broken branches as well as down for hoof-prints, Lindsey plunged into the woods. His mind raced ahead all the while. Atalanta, fleet-footed as her namesake, would doubtless have reached the stables by now, provided she met with no accident on her way. The arrival of their master's horse without their master in the saddle would prompt the grooms to send out a party to search for him. On horseback, they would catch Lindsey up with ease, and then he could enlist their services in helping him find Aubrey. And with their assistance, Aubrey would be found without delay.

Yet he couldn't quite keep from worrying about what Aubrey's condition might be once he was found.

Lightning strikes aside, horseback-riding was not without its perils, particularly as an inexperienced rider astride an out-of-control steed. Members of Lindsey's own hunt had snapped their spines riding neck-or-nothing within living memory. Aubrey might fall and break every bone in his body. Or he might fall out of the saddle without falling out of the stirrups, and be dragged along to bash his skull against every rock, root, and tree-trunk in the county. Or, even if he fell without catching his foot in the stirrups or cracking his head open upon impact, he might not roll out of Parsival's way in time to avoid being trampled underfoot. The number of disasters that could've befallen him in the time it took for the storm to pass seemed endless.

Still, Lindsey had found no blood or scraps of clothing or man-sized craters in the earth amongst the broken twigs and hoof-prints that marked Parsival's passing. Perhaps Aubrey had remained in the saddle after all. Perhaps Lindsey hadn't given him enough credit as a horseman. Perhaps all his worries were for nought.

The comforting thought had hardly passed through his mind before the sound of thunder again reached his ears.

No, not thunder. Hoofbeats.

Lindsey looked up sharp from the wet leaves just in time to see Parsival dashing towards him.

With an empty saddle.

Lindsey stared in hopeless shock. A panicked whinny from Parsival reminded him of his own danger. He ducked behind the broad trunk of an oak. The gelding dashed past, heedless of his master. Thundering hoofbeats echoed away into the incessant patter of the rain.

If Atalanta returning riderless didn't prompt the grooms to act, Parsival following close behind her with eyes rolling white and foam flying from his sides ought to spur them. Lindsey tried to take comfort in this as he forced his gaze away from where Parsival had gone and towards the path the gelding had taken to pass him.

Fresher tracks proved easier to follow. Less easy was the knowledge weighing upon Lindsey's mind, that Aubrey had indeed come unhorsed and now lay alone somewhere in the forest. Even Lindsey's ebullient optimism couldn't hope Aubrey had performed an emergency dismount similar to his own. And he had nothing but the noise of rain drizzling down through the leaves overhead to distract him from his fears.

Nothing but the rain, and another, softer sound, barely audible above the constant dripping of water, yet one which, once perceived, pierced Lindsey's hearing like the scream of a hawk.

The sound of a man calling out, "Who's there?"

Lindsey bolted upright. The voice—faint, weak, and tremulous though it might be—could only belong to his Aubrey.

"Aubrey?" he called back.

As moments passed without response, he feared he'd imagined the noise. Then, just on the edge of his hearing, came the most welcome sound of all. "Lindsey?"

Lindsey dashed ahead, but halted as he realised the crunching of leaves under his boots quite overpowered any other noise.

"Where are you?" he cried out instead.

He strained his ears for the answer and was rewarded with the reply, "Here. In the clearing. By the fallen log."

Lindsey glanced around for any of the landmarks Aubrey had named. The trees thinned ahead to the north, and corresponded with the disturbed leaves and branches marking Parsival's passing. He wasted no time in darting off towards them, leaping over tree-roots and stones in his path.

At last, the trees parted into a clearing ahead, and a fallen log lay within it, beside which Lindsey found a sight which sent his heart flying into his throat—the dark lump of a man crumpled upon the ground.

"Aubrey?" he gasped.

The lump shifted. A pale hand emerged to wave at him like a tattered banner above a parapet.

Lindsey ran.

Aubrey lay half-upright, propped on one arm against the fallen log. His features had gone bone-white and pulled into a grimace, and his gray suit had turned black with muck and rain, but his soft brown eyes focused upon Lindsey's with determination—and no small measure of relief.

Lindsey fell to his knees and embraced him.

~

Aubrey had never yet seen a more welcome sight than his Lindsey emerging from the woods and dashing to his rescue. The embrace that followed would have felt more welcome still, had it not aggravated his injuries. He tried to stifle his groan of pain. Evidently it didn't work, for Lindsey broke off the kiss abruptly to look down upon him with deep concern.

"Your head—" he began.

"Haven't hit it," Aubrey rushed to reassure him. Every breath felt like a knife in his ribs, yet he spoke on, wanting to banish the worried look from Lindsey's face. "Nor my back, neither. I tried to roll, like Fletcher told me, but I'm afraid I'm not much of a natural at it. Cracked a few things on the way down. But my head and neck are all right."

Lindsey looked very doubtful. His hands remained on Aubrey's face, and one thumb stroked his burnt cheek. The warmth of his palms radiated through Aubrey's rain-chilled skin. "What happened?"

"Parsival didn't take kindly to that lightning-strike. He bolted straight off. Did my best to stay on, and managed for a bit, but—" Aubrey shrugged, wincing at the resulting stab of pain through his shoulder and down his collarbone into his ribs. "Once he reached this damned log, he leapt over it and didn't quite take me with him. I'm just glad I got my boots out of the stirrups before I smashed my skull against it."

This last phrase had a disturbing effect upon Lindsey, whose face drained of colour as Aubrey spoke.

Aubrey, not wanting to dwell on his failures as a rider, hurried to change the subject. "What happened to you?"

"Much the same. Atalanta spooked, and by the time I'd got her under control, you were gone."

Lindsey's voice broke upon the last word, and Aubrey's heart with it. He hated to have caused so much distress in one he loved so dear.

"Well," said Aubrey, struggling to find something sufficient to comfort his Lindsey, to make amends. "You've found me."

It sounded lame to his own ears, but nevertheless, his efforts were rewarded with a bark of laughter from Lindsey, a sound as much cathartic relief as genuine joy.

Lindsey quickly stifled himself with a cough and resumed stroking Aubrey's rain-soaked hair. "Can you stand?"

"I think so, if you give me your arm."

Lindsey immediately rose and reached down to assist him. Aubrey clasped his proffered arm with both hands and struggled to his feet.

He held his breath as he did so, wary of the stabbing pain in his ribs that came with every breath. Despite this, he thought he managed rather well, until he put weight upon his left leg—at which point thunderbolts of agony shot through his ankle to lay him low. He'd have fallen entirely were it not for Lindsey's support. Lindsey, apparently readied in case Aubrey should collapse, swiftly ducked under Aubrey's arm and turned himself into a human crutch. The end result must have looked awkward, were there anyone around to see it, given the stark difference in their respective heights. Still, it allowed Aubrey to take the weight off his left leg and stand up. He leaned into Lindsey, who wrapped his arm snugly around him in response. Aubrey appreciated the gesture, though it was, perhaps, a little too snug for his ribcage.

Aubrey winced, sucking in a breath which only made the pain worse. "Not so tight."

Lindsey loosed his hold, but the furrows of concern in his brow only tightened. "Is your collarbone broken?"

"Ribs," Aubrey corrected him. "Cracked, not broken."

Lindsey appeared unconvinced. "We'll have to call on Dr Pilkington to make sure of that."

Aubrey didn't argue, though he well recognised the horrible grinding sensation. It felt the same as it had when he'd cracked his ribs in the Rook Mill explosion. Then, he'd had his burns to distract him from it. Now, his attention flitted freely between ribs and ankle as they scraped and throbbed in turn. He grit his chattering teeth, turned his mind to the strong clasp of Lindsey's hand on his arm, and leaned into his warm bulk as they limped back to the house together.

~

CHAPTER SIX

As Aubrey and Lindsey reached the road, they met with several of the household staff. Fletcher and the other grooms, along with Charles, had come out on horseback to search for the missing gentlemen. Fletcher caught sight of them first and immediately dismounted, leading his steed over to them and offering the reins to Lindsey.

"Glad to find you safe, sir," Fletcher blurted out.

It took Aubrey a moment to realise Fletcher had addressed not his employer, but Aubrey himself. Relief had only just begun to rub out the fretful lines in Fletcher's otherwise youthful features. The revelation that the groom had felt concern not just for Lindsey but for Aubrey as well left Aubrey feeling nothing less than astonished.

"Glad to be found," Aubrey managed after a moment of stunned silence.

His hacking cough put a stop to any further communication between them. Each cough stabbed through Aubrey's chest, the cracked ribs flaring with every reverberation. Even after his fit ended, he found it difficult to regather his breath, and the lack of it left him lightheaded—certainly in no position to climb on horseback. As Lindsey likewise refused to leave Aubrey's side, they were forced to stagger back to the house on foot, with the grooms riding around them like an escort of guards.

Lindsey sent Charles to telegram for Dr Pilkington immediately upon their return to the house. Even so, it took until evening for them to receive an answering telegram, and this only informed them that Dr Pilkington would arrive at the earliest possible hour tomorrow morning.

The hours in between sending for the surgeon and receiving a response passed quietly enough, if not without tension. Lindsey drew another hot bath for Aubrey, insisting it was necessary to warm his chilled bones. Aubrey didn't argue; he felt he needed it as much for the chill as for the mud splattered over him from head to toe.

"Another suit ruined," he reflected with some bitterness as Lindsey helped him undress.

Lindsey stopped in the midst of untying Aubrey's boot and looked up. "If that's the worst that's come of this, I'll be thankful."

There was something in his tone, not quite sharp, but more insistent than Aubrey was accustomed to hearing from him. Worried, that was it. No matter how Aubrey told him he was fine, cracked ribs and sprained ankle aside. Aubrey, used to harbouring all the anxiety in their relationship, felt uncomfortable at this shift in dynamics. "Sorry. I just—it feels like such a waste."

Lindsey's expression softened, and he stood to press a kiss to Aubrey's temple.

"Worth it," he whispered, "to have you home safe."

Aubrey swallowed down the lump in his throat and kissed him back.

Still, Lindsey's eyes lingered upon Aubrey's bruises far longer than they'd ever lingered upon his burn scars.

The second bath proved far less seductive than the first. The comfort of the warm water was off-set by the throbbing of Aubrey's bruises, the grinding of his cracked ribs, and the cough that had settled into his lungs as he lay out in the rain. He tried to suppress it, as not only did each hacking breath bring bolts of agony across his chest, but also deepened the concerned furrows in Lindsey's brow.

As he left the bath, Aubrey found himself shivering. Lindsey hurried to wrap him in a dressing gown warmed in front of the fire. Even so, Aubrey's teeth chattered as he leaned into Lindsey and staggered to bed. Bedsheets roasted with a warming-pan helped matters some, and Lindsey tucked additional quilts up over Aubrey's shoulders. Aubrey thought Lindsey might do still more to warm him up by slipping between the sheets himself, but as he opened his mouth to suggest it, he cut himself off with another hacking cough that cracked through his ribcage like gunshots, laying him low in breathless agonies.

Lindsey measured out a dose of laudanum, and for once, Aubrey didn't protest taking his medicine.

To help with the bitter taste of the laudanum, Lindsey had beef broth and toast brought up—an invalid's dinner. Aubrey stayed awake long enough to eat about half his portion. Then exhaustion forced him to push the remainder away. He didn't fall so much as collapse into sleep, losing consciousness before Lindsey could climb into bed beside him.

Hours later, Aubrey's own cough jolted him awake like a lightning strike through his ribcage.

In the dark, half-asleep, he fumbled with the laudanum bottle on the nightstand, the finicky dropper and the glass tumbler of water, to dispense a second dose. He held his breath all the while to stop the itch in his throat from turning into another cough and waking Lindsey—until a groan behind him told him he'd already failed.

"What..." Lindsey mumbled, even as Aubrey desperately prayed he'd fall back asleep. Then came the sounds of Lindsey fumbling with the nightstand on his own side of the bed, the drawer rattling open and shut, and the hiss of a struck match flaring to life. The soft glow of candlelight suffused the room, revealing Lindsey's befuddled expression, and Aubrey's secret medicinal shame.

Aubrey had never felt more like an opium-eater. "Go back to sleep," he meant to say, but the moment he let air pass over his vocal chords, his throat contracted, and he lost all words in coughing.

Lindsey set down the candle, reached over Aubrey, and took over dispensing the laudanum, tossing out the water Aubrey had failed with and beginning afresh from the pitcher. Aubrey witnessed less than half his work, his coughing fit forcing his eyes shut. Then he felt Lindsey's hand settle upon his back and heard a gentle voice bid, "Drink this," and opened his eyes to find Lindsey looking upon him with an expression equal parts exhaustion and concern, holding the tumbler up to his face.

Aubrey raised a shaking hand to join Lindsey's in clasping the glass and tipped it down his own ungrateful throat with perhaps more force than advisable for an invalid.

They fell back into bed, but Aubrey could not fall asleep. Every time his eyes fell shut, his sore throat would itch and his lungs convulse, and the resulting stab like a spear in his side would jolt him awake again. In desperation he grabbed a pillow and clutched it to his ribs to absorb even a fraction of the shock that rattled his ribcage with every breath. It helped some, and combined with the laudanum, allowed him eventual sleep.

The next morning found Aubrey's ankle much better. The swelling had nearly gone, and only a slight limp remained in his gait. His ribs, however, felt as bad as the day before, and the lost sleep didn't help matters.

Fortunately, Dr Pilkington came on the first train. Aubrey had just finished breakfast—in bed, at Lindsey's insistence—when Charles announced the return of the family carriage to the drive, and Dr Pilkington came into the sickroom.

After a perfunctory examination of Aubrey's ankle, Dr Pilkington declared it had merely "rolled," not sprained and certainly not broken, despite Lindsey's concerns. Then the stethoscope came out of the black leather bag, and Dr Pilkington warmed it against his palm while Aubrey reluctantly disrobed just enough to allow for an examination of his ribs. Dr Pilkington listened intently to Aubrey's breathing. Aubrey wondered if his stethoscope allowed him to hear the grinding of the bones as well.

"Hairline fractures," Dr Pilkington declared as he removed the buds from his ears. "The cough concerns me, but there's no crackling, which means no pneumonia as of yet. I'd still like to keep a close watch on your lungs as matters develop. In the meantime, I strongly caution against bed-rest."

Aubrey, who'd rather expected to hear the exact opposite recommendation, raised his brows.

Lindsey likewise appeared surprised and a great deal more perturbed. "No bed-rest?"

"No bed-rest," Dr Pilkington confirmed, rolling up his stethoscope and slipping it back into his bag. "If we're to keep pneumonia out of your lungs, Mr Warren, then you need to continue breathing as normally as you can manage. That's the danger of broken ribs. Shallow breathing allows for fluid to build up, and pneumonia settles in. So you must make a conscious effort at deep-breathing, at least once per hour. I can recommend laudanum for cough-suppression, and for the pain, but I must insist you get out of bed as much as you can stand, and breathe deep!"

Aubrey, who'd been dreading the prospect of lying about for weeks on end, struggled to withhold his joy at this prescription. "I'll do my best."

"See that you do," replied Dr Pilkington. "I'd like to return to check on your progress at the end of the week. But don't hesitate to send for me if you feel any worse."

With that, he stood up to leave. Lindsey rose as well and, with a concerned glance back at Aubrey, showed the doctor out. As they departed, Aubrey caught a snatch of conversation.

"If I might have a word…" came Lindsey's hushed tones.

The creak of the door falling shut overpowered the rest.

~

Lindsey had hoped Dr Pilkington's arrival would soothe his own worries along with Aubrey's wounds. Instead, he found himself more worried than ever.

"Are you sure," he said in hushed tones as he escorted the surgeon down to the foyer, "there is no cause for concern?"

"No more than usual," Dr Pilkington replied easily. "Certainly far less than when last I treated him."

Lindsey well recalled that prior meeting between his Aubrey and the good doctor. He'd first consulted Dr Pilkington on Graves's recommendation, when Aubrey, returning home from Withington Hospital, had suffered morphine withdrawals on top of the injuries he'd incurred in the boiler explosion at Rook Mill.

"Do not allow him to stay abed," Dr Pilkington continued, drawing Lindsey out of his troubling reminiscences. "Ensure he does his breathing exercises and remains otherwise active."

"Should he get back on the horse, as well?" Lindsey asked in disbelief.

Dr Pilkington chuckled. "Not quite yet. Though some light perambulation around the house and grounds would do him good. You needn't worry about him unless that cough of his grows worse, or unless it starts bringing up mucus. Should either occur, send for me without delay."

They'd reached the front courtyard by then, so Lindsey could do little more than promise to follow doctor's orders and let him return to London. He watched the family carriage rattle away down the drive towards the village and the train station, then returned to the house and took the stairs two at a time back to his bedroom.

All the while, he tried to reconcile Dr Pilkington's advice with his own instincts. He knew Dr Pilkington as an able and trustworthy surgeon, whose advice and expertise had already saved Aubrey's life once before. Still, Lindsey couldn't quite silence the little nagging voice in the back of his mind which fretted for Aubrey's sake. This little nagging voice only grew louder once he opened the bedroom door.

The bed was empty.

Lindsey stared at the spot where he'd left his Aubrey not a quarter-hour ago. The bed wasn't just empty—it was made-up, as if whoever had left it had no intention of returning anytime soon, or indeed, had never been there. Aubrey's pyjamas were folded neatly at the foot of the bed, ready for the maid to collect for laundry. Aubrey himself, however, had totally vanished.

A glance into the bathroom did not reveal Aubrey. Nor did the journey into the hall, or down the grand staircase in the foyer. In the breakfast-room, Lindsey found not Aubrey, but Charles, who informed him Aubrey had gone down to the ballroom with Halloway.

Lindsey did not run to the ballroom, though it took great presence of mind to keep from doing so. He paused before the double doors to gather himself. From within, he heard muted conversation, a few notes of Halloway's laughter, and a cough from Aubrey. Lindsey flexed his hands to steady himself, then pushed open the door.

Halloway stood in front of his easel, arranging the tools of his trade, stripped down to his rolled-up shirtsleeves. Aubrey stood beside him, clad in his dressing gown and slippers, his everyday suit folded up and set aside near the pile of pillows, crates, and tarps.

"Aubrey!" said Lindsey, cutting off whatever conversation passed between them. He just barely stopped himself from adding, *Shouldn't you be in bed?*

Aubrey had already turned to regard him upon his entrance and appeared no less puzzled now. "Yes?"

"What are you doing here?" Lindsey asked.

This question did nothing to clear up the bewildered expression on Aubrey's face. "Modelling for Halloway."

Lindsey cast about for the most diplomatic phrasing possible. "Are you certain that's a wise course of action, given your injuries?"

"Dr Pilkington warned against bed rest," Aubrey reminded him. "And this will hardly tax me."

Lindsey, helpless, turned to Halloway for reinforcement.

Halloway coughed. "Forgive me for being indelicate, but given how Warren's wounds were sustained in a fall... They could add great verisimilitude to my work."

Lindsey stared at Halloway.

"In that case," Aubrey piped up, "I ought to return to modelling without delay. Otherwise the bruising won't be fresh and the colours will turn."

Lindsey stared at Aubrey.

"Fresh bruises would be ideal," Halloway agreed.

Lindsey gave up staring at both of them, instead casting his gaze upon the painting-in-progress. Even in his distracted state, he had to concede the work had compelling properties. The pose of Icarus showed off Aubrey's body to great advantage and made his natural beauty impossible to ignore.

Meanwhile, the voice of the flesh-and-blood Aubrey broke into Lindsey's considerations. "Did you want to stay and supervise the proceedings?"

Since the beginning of the artistic process, Lindsey had felt intense curiosity and intrigue regarding the painting. He'd held back out of respect for Aubrey's sensibilities and for Halloway's work. Now, invited to act the part of the voyeur, he found the suggestion allayed many of his concerns. He needn't spend the day fretting in ignorance; if anything dreadful should befall Aubrey in the course of modelling, he'd be first to know of it, and better still, be perfectly positioned to render aid.

"I'd very much like to," Lindsey admitted. He cast a glance at Halloway. "That is, if you don't object...?"

Halloway shrugged. "Not in the least. Shall we?"

An extra chair was brought in from the dining room, along with the laudanum bottle from the bedroom, at Lindsey's request. The ballroom doors shut tight against prying eyes from within. Halloway added fresh paint to his palette. All was readiness.

Aubrey stepped out of his slippers and made as if to resume his pose—then paused, with a glance at Lindsey. Their eyes locked for an instant.

Lindsey smiled at him, a simple, supportive gesture.

Aubrey returned it in his usual way—a shy flicker, hardly more than a twitch of his lips, yet providing such warmth in its brief flash as to melt the heart of any man who saw it.

Then he let the silk robe slip off his shoulders in a singular shrug—and handed the article over to Lindsey in a manner as shy as his previous gesture had been bold.

Lindsey took it, letting his hand clasp Aubrey's within the robe's folds as he did so, a quick squeeze of assurance.

Aubrey bit back a second smile as, together, they approached the makeshift background. Coming up to it, Lindsey perceived the charcoal outline of a body laid out over the draped canvas tarps. Aubrey started to settle in to the position indicated by the markings—then stopped with an abrupt wince. Lindsey offered his arm, and Aubrey took it with evident gratitude. With Lindsey's help, he lowered himself down into place.

Halloway, from his post by his easel, called out for a few minor adjustments of Aubrey's position. Then he declared himself ready to begin, and Lindsey, with some reluctance, had only to "step out of frame," as it were.

Lindsey returned to his chair beside Halloway's easel and settled in to watch the proceedings.

He had seen Aubrey nude before, of course—many times over. But never quite from this perspective. When Aubrey disrobed behind their bedroom door, for example, he was always within Lindsey's reach, and often helping to undress Lindsey in turn. Lindsey could run an idle hand over the wiry muscles of his arms—astonishing to see when Aubrey removed his shirt and revealed how the narrow frame beneath his suit held unforeseen strength—or trace his fingertips through the dusting of fine black hairs across his chest, and trail them down to the matching line over his belly, leading further south to the soft black curls nestled around his prick. He could smooth his thumbs over the jutting points of Aubrey's hipbones, or grasp the shapely thighs and feel them tremble beneath his ministrations, or caress the sharp definition of his calves. He could kiss the spread of burn scars from cheek to shoulder, arm to fingertip, and show how he valued the marks of survival, ingenuity, and courage.

Now, he could do nothing more than stare.

The painting had transformed Lindsey from tactile lover to wistful voyeur. At present, only his eyes could roam over the curve of Aubrey's collarbone or the slender bend of his waist. The distance heightened Lindsey's appreciation for the beloved and familiar form before him.

Even so, the bruises were new.

Lindsey had seen them yesterday in the dim gaslight of their bedroom and the bath. The sight of them had stopped his heart, had required a sharp intake of breath to fortify himself against exclaiming aloud in alarm. Then, they had appeared like blotches of deep crimson watercolour blooming across Aubrey's parchment-pale skin. Now, a day later, they had turned a dreadful shade of blue-black, like indigo ink, as dark as the night sky absent of moon and stars and hope. The mass over Aubrey's ribcage looked the worst, marking out where the three ribs had cracked, from whence the greatest portion of his pain stemmed, and had kept them both awake half the night.

With neither bedsheets nor robe to shield them from view, Lindsey saw every hitch in Aubrey's breath, every flinch and wince, every cough reverberating throughout his frame, every tremulous, half-imagined shifting of his cracked ribs beneath the brutal bloom of his bruises.

Lindsey wanted nothing more than to fold Aubrey's broken and battered form within his arms, to clasp him in a warm embrace, to shield him from further harm.

But he could only watch.

Lindsey tore his eyes away from the painful visual reminder of Aubrey's suffering and turned them instead towards Halloway and his canvas.

The painting, which had looked almost as good as finished to Lindsey's amateur eyes, proved barely begun. Halloway built up layer upon layer of brush-strokes, blending in new and more exacting hues, bringing the image of *Icarus Fallen* into sharper focus like a photographer adjusting his lens by minute degrees.

So too did the new bruises come into focus. At first Halloway added stark dashes of maroon, crimson, and indigo on top of what had initially appeared as a completed painting of unblemished flesh. Then the blending began, and sharp edges of the paint daubs faded into a more lifelike representation of Aubrey's very real contusions. Every delicate flick of the bristles brought new life into Icarus, making the fallen form seem to breathe within the confines of the canvas, as if actual blood flowed beneath painted skin.

Halloway talked as he painted, with the same easygoing air he always had at dinner parties and more casual gatherings. At first he directed his gentle enquiries at Aubrey—out of habit, from what Lindsey could gather—before the pained tones of Aubrey's replies checked him, and he instead turned his conversational prowess upon Lindsey. If pressed for details afterwards, Lindsey would be unable to tell what, exactly, the topics of their discourse had been, or how they had flowed from one into the other. He knew only that it felt friendly and carefree as ever.

Awe-inspiring though he found Halloway's speed and skill, Lindsey couldn't help stealing glances at his Aubrey. One of these glances caught Aubrey's eye and earned him a shy half-smile. Lindsey returned it, wishing all the while he could press his hand to his cheek and feel the smile against his palm, whilst Aubrey, as he so often did, disguised his evident pleasure with a kiss to Lindsey's wrist.

As he watched, Lindsey twisted Aubrey's robe around his hands in his lap. The silk folds still felt warm. He hoped Aubrey wasn't too cold without it.

~

CHAPTER SEVEN

While Aubrey still didn't consider modelling terribly labour-intensive compared to some of his previous careers, it nevertheless proved trying to his bruised and broken body. Laudanum reduced the frequency and violence of his coughing fits, but it could not eliminate them entirely, and every time he coughed, it took some minutes to settle back into the correct position.

Aubrey apologised the first time it happened, which earned him a confused look from Lindsey and a shrug from Halloway.

"Don't worry about it," Halloway said, unruffled as ever.

The second time it occurred, Aubrey apologised again.

Again, Halloway told him not to worry about it, and added, "It's not as though you're doing it on purpose."

Aubrey gave up apologising, though the coughing fits continued throughout the morning. While not an artist himself, he could well imagine how difficult it must be to have the position of one's model shifting violently every other minute. Still, Halloway never once complained, nor displayed the least hint of annoyance.

Lindsey, meanwhile, had developed a semi-permanent crease of concern between his brows.

It felt awkward to have Lindsey watching, if not quite for the reasons Aubrey had expected. After all, Lindsey had seen him nude more times than either of them could count, and out of all the people who'd witnessed Aubrey's naked body, Lindsey was by far the most appreciative of the sight. Even the combination of Lindsey and Halloway's presence, the intimate mingling with the merely observant, proved not so bad as Aubrey had anticipated when he first suggested Lindsey stay to watch. Aubrey had resigned himself to soldiering on through whatever uncomfortable moments would doubtless ensue—a small price to pay for Lindsey's peace of mind.

Halloway, however, swooped in to their rescue. His easy conversation continued just as if they all sat together in the library with their clothes very much on. His words did wonders towards dispersing the cloud of tension looming over the ballroom. Aubrey marvelled at it, and at length, had to conclude that Halloway had some experience with painting couples. Or at the very least, experience in handling husbands watching to make sure their wives weren't getting too friendly with the portrait artist.

Yet there remained one problem with Lindsey's presence. Whenever the conversation came to a natural lull, or whenever he thought himself unobserved, his eyes came to rest again and again upon Aubrey's bruises. And even when he wasn't staring at the ugly contusions spreading across Aubrey's chest, he looked extremely worried.

Aubrey wished he could assuage Lindsey's evident fears, but truth told, he felt as wretched as Lindsey obviously thought he looked. Even with the laudanum, following doctor's orders to "breathe deep" proved easier said than done. Each attempt provoked another repressed coughing fit and left him weaker than the last. When he'd first disrobed this morning, he'd felt chilled by the slight draught through the windows Halloway had opened for ventilation. By noon, the ballroom felt as stuffy and overheated as if a hundred dancing couples whirled within it. And yet, despite the intense warmth, Aubrey still shivered.

At last they broke for luncheon. It took Aubrey a few attempts to rise from his reclining position. In the meantime, Lindsey leapt from his chair and strode towards Aubrey to deliver his robe. Aubrey, who had managed to stand by the time Lindsey arrived despite the latter's hurry, reached out to accept it. As he did so, he saw his own hand trembled with no small violence.

Lindsey noticed as well—his blue eyes flying wide for an instant before he checked his alarm—and changed his approach, shaking the robe out and holding it up before him, its open front towards Aubrey.

Aubrey gave him a weak smile in silent thanks as he turned and slid his arms into the sleeves of the garment. Lindsey tugged it up over his shoulders before he could even think to shrug. Then, placing his hand on the small of Aubrey's back, he gently guided him to the chair where he'd put all his clothes; his jacket and waistcoat draped over the back, the shirt, trousers, and small-clothes folded in a tidy stack on the seat. Aubrey, still shivering, attempted to dress himself, but his shaking hands fumbled in their grasp upon his shirt. All the while he felt Lindsey's concerned gaze upon him.

"I'm fine," Aubrey asserted through gritted teeth, to no one in particular.

Lindsey didn't appear convinced. He seemed about to suggest Aubrey needn't get dressed at all, which was ludicrous. Aubrey couldn't face the notion of stepping out into the hallway, where any passing member of the staff might glimpse him, in only a dressing gown. Footmen and maids alike despised his burnt face. They would think no better of the scars trailing down his collar to his side and arm, visible by turns in the ever-shifting silk of the robe. Liminal spaces like the corridors and staircases of the Wiltshire house posed the greatest threat to Aubrey's dignity. He had no wish to face them without the armour of his suit.

Still, Lindsey said nothing of it as he unfolded each of Aubrey's garments in turn and held them out for him to shrug on or step into. His deft fingers did up buttons, buckled garters, smoothed his lapels, knotted his tie, and turned down his collar with tender finesse. In a matter of moments, Aubrey stood as ready as any man not shaking like a leaf in a hurricane, beset by coughing fits.

"Go on ahead," said Halloway, in the midst of cleaning his brushes with turpentine. "I'll catch you up shortly."

In the hallway they encountered Charles, who had come to tell them their meal was ready. Lindsey thanked him and added instruction for a fire to be built up in the dining room.

"I'm not cold," Aubrey began to protest through chattering teeth, but a cough broke through the last word, and took some moments to pass, leaving him doubled over breathless with stabbing pains in his side.

When it ended, Lindsey had a firm arm around his shoulders and used it to help Aubrey pull himself upright against him. The moment Aubrey stood, Lindsey had the back of his elegant hand pressed against Aubrey's brow. The gentle gesture nevertheless sparked pinpricks of pain, and Aubrey winced at the shock of Lindsey's cold flesh on his burning skin.

Lindsey dropped his hand. "Perhaps you ought to have luncheon in bed."

Aubrey's pride demanded he argue. But in his weakened state, he bit his tongue and admitted defeat with a nod.

The journey from the ballroom on the ground floor to the bedroom upstairs took a still greater toll on Aubrey's body. By the time they arrived on the threshold, he remained standing only by virtue of Lindsey's assistance. Lindsey half-carried him to the bed. Aubrey collapsed upon it as much in relief as exhaustion. He could make only the barest effort to assist Lindsey in undressing him, undoing all the work they'd done just minutes before. But when Lindsey made to pull the bedclothes up over his shoulders, Aubrey shook his head.

"I'm too warm by half already," he croaked out, earning himself another coughing assault upon his ribcage.

Lindsey relented and opened a window.

The day passed in a feverish haze. Aubrey had only intermittent impressions of the world around him—a damp flannel pressed against his forehead; a teacup against his lips, and the soothing sensation of tea with lemon flowing down his raw throat, its flavour not quite covering the bitter taste of laudanum; the sound of Lindsey's voice telling Charles to send for Dr Pilkington.

Dr Pilkington arrived in the evening. Despite his efforts to warm his stethoscope through friction against his palm, the shock of cold metal against Aubrey's burning skin prompted a gasp which became another coughing fit. Dr Pilkington listened throughout, and, after coaxing Aubrey to try breathing in again as deep as he could manage, made his grim diagnosis: pneumonia.

The cold prick of the thermometer under Aubrey's tongue confirmed his fever had reached worrisome proportions. Next he knew, Lindsey had lifted him out of bed and half-carried him to the bath, filled with lukewarm water under Dr Pilkington's direction. Immersion offered relief beyond expression. All too soon the tub was drained, and Aubrey stood, however briefly, naked and shivering, the blaze of fever chasing the cold draughts across his skin. Then flannel bandages soaked in cold water were wrapped snug around his ribcage—the stabbing pains of his ribs no less acute for their familiarity—and at last a robe was thrown over his shoulders before Lindsey guided him back to bed. Another dose of opium, this time in the form of morphine tablets for cough suppression, and Aubrey found himself almost able to drift off.

Dr Pilkington murmured to Lindsey some minutes later, apparently operating under the assumption Aubrey had already fallen asleep, "Has he done any strenuous activity since I saw him this morning?"

A moment's hesitation passed before Lindsey replied, "He has modelled for a painting."

Aubrey didn't have the strength to open his eyes, but the pause following Lindsey's answer bespoke surprise on the doctor's part. He wished circumstances had not required Lindsey to give an honest answer. From what Aubrey knew of Dr Pilkington—that he came under recommendation from Graves, and that Graves had identified him as a fellow invert—he doubted anything he or Lindsey might do or say could shock him. Surely he had treated Graves and others for more bizarre afflictions, and under circumstances much more questionable than modelling for a painting. Still, Aubrey's pride did not go down easy.

"At the risk of being indelicate," Dr Pilkington said at last, "I'd like to know the particulars."

Over the course of the next few excruciating minutes, Lindsey confirmed Aubrey had modelled in the nude, the makeshift studio was well-ventilated, and the pose was indeed a reclining one.

"Do you think it too vigorous?" Lindsey asked.

"On the contrary," Dr Pilkington replied. "I'm afraid it's not vigorous enough. While I would not have recommended Mr Warren spend the morning naked in a draughty room, it would have given me less concern had he performed some exercise whilst doing so—a brisk walk, or some more aerobic activity, something to keep himself active and warm. But to stay quite still for so long, and to recline whilst doing so… I'm afraid that is as bad as bed-rest. Worse, for the lack of anything to insulate him from the chill."

Aubrey privately supposed he'd have been better off going straight back to the stables.

Lindsey remained with him well into the night, sitting beside the bed rather than climbing in beside Aubrey. Aubrey felt torn between wishing for Lindsey's arms around him and knowing how the warmth radiating from Lindsey's body would only make his fever more unbearable. Still, the clasp of Lindsey's hand in his own, the gentle mopping of his brow, and the murmured reassurances from Lindsey's lips made the hours pass far more comfortably than they would've otherwise. Aubrey only wished Lindsey could find rest of his own.

By morning, the combined efforts of Charles, Halloway, and Dr Pilkington convinced Lindsey to leave Aubrey's side and go to bed in some other room, however briefly.

In the wake of Lindsey's departure came the arrival of the oxygen.

It took considerable effort of Aubrey's fever-addled brain to put together the scraps of the story he could overhear from the conversation above and around his bed, but from what he could gather, Dr Pilkington, upon diagnosing pneumonia the previous evening, had ordered several cylinders of compressed oxygen delivered to the Wiltshire house. Certain limitations, such as having to send away to a mining supplier for the oxygen, had delayed the delivery until morning. The moment Aubrey realised what Dr Pilkington had brought into his sickroom, he bolted upright—or rather, made a valiant attempt at doing so.

"You needn't be alarmed, Mr Warren," Dr Pilkington reassured him, laying gentle-yet-firm hands upon his shoulders to push him back down into a reclining position. "It will assist your breathing."

"I know," Aubrey wheezed. He'd read all about the new and life-saving use of compressed oxygen in *The Engineer*, particularly in rescuing miners overcome by pockets of suffocating gas deep beneath the earth. "I only want to see the mechanism."

His difficulty in gathering breath rather muted the enthusiasm he wished to express, but Dr Pilkington seemed to understand his intentions nonetheless.

Aubrey, his eyes bright with excitement as well as fever, watched as Dr Pilkington raised the oxygen to his field of vision and began laying out the pieces required for its administration, briefly explaining the function of each in turn; the cylinder of compressed oxygen itself, its outlet controlled by a key; the small rubber bag; the quart wash-bottle; the supple rubber hose and the hard-rubber nose-piece. Dr Pilkington then filled the wash-bottle one-third of the way with water, assembled all the disparate pieces into the singular apparatus, and inserted the nose-piece into Aubrey's nostrils. This last could not be called comfortable under any circumstances, but Aubrey found his discomfort tempered by his own fascination as the oxygen, released from the cylinder, bubbled its way across the water in the wash-bottle to the rubber hose and into Aubrey's lungs, providing no small measure of relief to his laboured breathing. At long last, as the light of dawn spread across the room from between the fluttering curtains at the open window, Aubrey found something like sleep.

When he next awoke, daylight remained, and Lindsey had returned, sitting beside his bed looking haggard.

Aubrey smiled to see him despite his worry at his appearance. "Did Dr Pilkington show you the oxygen?"

Lindsey didn't seem quite so elated as Aubrey felt at the mention of the intriguing new mechanism. "He did. Is it helping?"

Aubrey noted how Lindsey's concerned gaze traced over the rubber tubing from the iron cylinder to his nose and back again. He tempered some of his enthusiasm. "I feel much better rested already. Perhaps we should have some for you as well."

Lindsey chuckled and gave Aubrey's hand a brief yet heartfelt squeeze. "If the doctor prescribes it, I suppose I shall have to submit."

Even with his mind addled by fever and exhaustion, Aubrey knew his illness had robbed Lindsey of his bed, and his respite along with it. He pushed down his guilt to ask, "Where have you been sleeping?"

"One of the guest rooms. It's not far," Lindsey hurried to reassure him—unnecessarily so, but Aubrey appreciated it nonetheless. He liked to know Lindsey hadn't flown too far off, despite his worries that his coughing carried through the walls and kept Lindsey awake. "Dr Pilkington wouldn't let me stay."

"You need to sleep, too," Aubrey reminded him, though his tremulous voice weakened his argument.

"I have," Lindsey promised him. "Though I'll sleep far better when I'm beside you again."

Aubrey, already exhausted even by such brief conversation, concentrated all he wished to say of his gratitude and his affections into a strong clasp of Lindsey's hand. Lindsey kissed his knuckles, and Aubrey knew he'd been heard.

"Go back to sleep," Lindsey murmured.

Aubrey, too weak to do otherwise, obeyed.

He awoke to dusk, and a tray laden with tea-things and a bowl of beef broth. Lindsey laid out the invalid's dinner as smartly as a table-setting at one of Rowena's parties, smoothing a napkin like a tablecloth over Aubrey's bared collar and breastbone. His strong arm wound its way around Aubrey's shoulders and lifted him ever-so-gently into a sitting position. One soft palm cupped the back of Aubrey's head whilst the other supported Aubrey's own trembling grip on the spoon and raised it to his fever-cracked lips. The warm, rich broth soothed Aubrey's sore throat as it flowed down. Still, he could only manage two-thirds of the bowl before exhaustion overtook him again, and with another dose of morphine tablets, he drifted off.

When next he opened his eyes, daylight had returned—mid-morning, by his guess. Lindsey had gone, and in his place, Aubrey found Dr Pilkington. The usual battery of stethoscope and thermometer occurred, along with a renewal of the oxygen.

"Your fever has reduced," Dr Pilkington informed him conversationally. "With any luck, you'll shake this off in a few days, so long as you continue to rest."

Aubrey reluctantly acquiesced to this prescription. He did feel stronger, until he made a fool's effort to lift not only his head but also his shoulders from the pillow, at which point his cracked ribs gave him a sharp reminder to lie still.

The oxygen tube made his limited breathing more productive, and the morphine tablets reduced his cough, but the grinding of bones and the crackling in his lungs remained. Aubrey slept away most of the next few days, rejoicing any moment he opened his eyes to Lindsey beside him. Otherwise his visitors were limited to Dr Pilkington, with assistance from Charles—Aubrey supposed allowances had to be made for when one couldn't move for fractures and fevers, and he didn't protest Charles stepping in whilst Lindsey caught some much-needed rest.

On one occasion, however, he woke to the sound of a woman's voice. At first, his muddled mind protested that Rowena and Emmeline remained in Paris, and thus the sound of a woman's voice in the Wiltshire house made no sense at all. Yet as Dr Pilkington's sober tones answered her, and she spoke on in halting syllables, he caught enough of her speech to recognise the Welsh accent of Miss Owen.

Aubrey struggled against the laudanum to open his eyes and

managed at last a glimpse from under his lashes. Both Dr Pilkington and Miss Owen stood by his bedside, the former instructing the latter in nursing duties for the invalid. Dr Pilkington held one of the oxygen canisters, and Miss Owen had said something which gave him evident pause.

"You are familiar with the mechanism?" Dr Pilkington asked her at last.

"I've seen it used," Miss Owen admitted. "My family all work in the mines."

She didn't need to elaborate which mines. Given her knowledge of the canisters and her Welsh accent, Aubrey felt safe to assume her kin worked in coal. He wondered, then, what had brought her to such a house as this, in a far different career, but he hadn't the energy to open his eyes, much less the breath to voice such questions. And so he slipped back down into sleep with his mysteries.

Many days passed in the patchwork sleeping-and-waking cycle before it occurred to Aubrey to wonder what became of Halloway. He did so to himself at first, then aloud to Lindsey at the first opportunity.

"He's still here," Lindsey assured him. "He wishes you a rapid recovery. Dr Pilkington says you're not strong enough for visitors just yet—he's hardly letting me in as it is—but the moment you're feeling more yourself, you may see him."

"How long before I'm permitted to model for him again?" Aubrey joked.

His humour didn't quite hit the mark, judging by the flicker of alarm across Lindsey's features. But Lindsey recovered himself with a handsome, if somewhat forced, smile. "Another month at least, I'm afraid. Likely two."

Aubrey promised Lindsey he was content to wait.

As it turned out, he had to wait ten whole days before Dr Pilkington felt confident enough in his continued survival to leave the Wiltshire house.

"Keep him in bed," Dr Pilkington urged Lindsey for the fourth time as he made his good-byes. "And if any symptom should grow in the least bit worse, do not hesitate to send for me again. I will return without delay."

Lindsey swore a solemn oath to do so, over Aubrey's silent protest that such a thing would probably not prove necessary.

Later that afternoon, when Lindsey nodded off in his chair at Aubrey's bedside, Charles and Aubrey combined forces to coax Lindsey to go rest elsewhere. Not a quarter-hour after Lindsey reluctantly departed, Halloway sidled into the room.

Aubrey sat up—he could do so at last, with his fever broken, and the shooting pains in his side muffled by a combination of morphine tablets and strategic pillows—all eagerness to see him. Yet Halloway remained muted, settling into the chair beside Aubrey's bed with some unknown shadow dulling his smile.

"How are you getting on, then?" Aubrey asked him. His voice remained thin and reedy, but he could get through a whole sentence without coughing.

Halloway's reply—"Well enough."—sounded a far cry from the ebullient-if-dry *raconteur* Aubrey had come to know over the course of their collaboration.

Aubrey tried again. "Have you got much painting done?"

At the mention of his craft, a spark came into Halloway's eyes. "A little. Some watercolour sketches of the house and grounds."

"Any progress on *Icarus Fallen*?"

The stricken look on Halloway's face made Aubrey think some dreadful accident had destroyed the potential masterpiece.

"I tried," Halloway said. "It's mostly done on your end—all but the finer details of the portraiture—and I started in on the wings—but—"

He broke off and looked out the window. His hand, its fingers still stained with smears of paint, ran through his hair, then on down his face. He smoothed down his moustache three times, only to then begin worrying one side of it between two fingers, creating a lopsided curl. At last, he met Aubrey's gaze again.

"Rather hard to concentrate," Halloway admitted. "Knowing it nearly killed you."

Aubrey stared. He hadn't expected such concern from one so carefree and Bohemian. It touched him, certainly. Still, some facts had to be corrected. "It's not the painting's fault that I misinterpreted doctor's orders. Will you agree to share the blame, at least?"

Halloway stared at him—then a second smile, broader and more sincere than the first, broke through his overcast expression. "Only if you let me apologise properly."

Aubrey conceded to this condition with a nod.

Halloway clasped Aubrey's hand and leaned in. "I'm sorry for my part in all this. I never meant to make you ill, and it was foolish of me not to foresee the obvious conclusion of such a business."

"You're forgiven," Aubrey blurted the instant he'd finished.

Halloway released his hand with a laugh and leaned back in the bedside chair, almost as carefree as he'd appeared before. "Fair enough."

A sudden suspicion occurred to Aubrey, preventing him from sharing in Halloway's good humour for the moment. "Lindsey hasn't given you any trouble over the matter, has he?"

"Not in the least," Halloway scoffed. "Though I wouldn't blame him if he did. Truth told, he's been far too preoccupied looking after you to bother me or anyone else." He paused, a wistful smile ghosting over his face. "He's a damned good man, is your Lindsey."

Aubrey, choked by something more than his illness, took a moment to make his reply. "I've often thought so." Thinking of Lindsey sparked a reminder in his mind, and he sat up a hair further in bed. "Halloway—you said you're nearly done with the painting? Would you be willing to take on a commission? Or a pair of them, I suppose."

Halloway raised an eager eyebrow. "I'm always interested in commissions. What did you have in mind?"

With a looseness of tongue he would later blame on the laudanum, Aubrey described the theoretical commissions. Halloway's curious smile became a conspiratorial one.

~

That evening, after ten whole wretched nights apart, Lindsey finally slid into bed beside Aubrey, with an embrace none the less enthusiastic for all its tender care. Aubrey returned it with the desperation of a drowning man clasping his rescuer. Without the damned rubber tubing between them, he breathed in Lindsey's masculine scent, its familiar notes soothing his heartache better than the morphine soothed the ache in his ribs.

"I've missed you," Lindsey whispered into his hair, echoing Aubrey's own thoughts.

Aubrey answered him with a kiss before nestling his head into the hollow of Lindsey's collar, precisely where he belonged.

~

CHAPTER EIGHT

The relief Lindsey felt in that moment—to have his Aubrey safe again in his arms at last—could hardly be expressed in words. He fell asleep cradling his frail form and awoke better-rested than he'd felt in almost a fortnight.

Charles brought up breakfast—a proper breakfast, with toast and bacon and eggs and scones and muffins and ham and every other sundry the cook could dream up, all of which Dr Pilkington had at last given permission to re-introduce to the invalid's diet. Lindsey watched with satisfaction as Aubrey joined him in devouring it.

Alongside the breakfast-tray came a silver salver of correspondence. Lindsey set aside the latest issue of *The Strand* and flipped through the letters. A particular pair of envelopes caught his attention—one addressed to himself, in his sister's hand, and one addressed to Aubrey, in his *fiancée*'s. He handed over Aubrey's letter with a knowing smile and opened his own with a deft slash.

Dearest Lindsey,

Emmeline's trousseau is coming along slowly but surely. I have tried thus far in vain to convince her to give up the notion of a chartreuse wedding gown. To the hue itself I have no real objection, apart from a sense of taste, but the chemical composition is known for its detrimental effect upon the health of the wearer, which must give one pause. If she insists on garbing herself in Parisian green every day, I fear she will make you a widower within a year of your marriage. Or perhaps a grain or two will drop from her skirts into your tea and leave her with a handsome inheritance. Regardless, I promise you I will redouble my efforts to make her a less literal "*killing creature.*"

Disputes over colour aside, I can assure you my guidance has given her a wardrobe both flattering and fashionable. You needn't fear your bride embarrassing you in that regard. And I hope you won't mind my addition of a few articles of my own to her account. I feel it's a fair price for the continual head-ache she has given me over this past fortnight—but she's an innocent darling, and means none of it.

When not supervising her choices in the House of Worth, I, along with my dear Lady Pelham, have spent my mornings, afternoons, evenings, and nights chaperoning your fiancée *all over Paris to visit every single technological marvel or engineering feat or scientific exhibition she can discover. You'll be happy to hear she finds a great deal of joy in them. I, on the other hand, have absorbed not one single word of scientific enrichment. Instead, I have acquired a much deeper understanding of what is truly meant by the French idea of* ennui. *I have also, by exercising every inch of cunning I possess to its fullest extreme, convinced her to attend some more artistic programmes—the museums, the galleries, the* salons, *and even a few private tours of painters' and sculptors' studios—but she appears as immune to the arts as I am to the sciences. The effort has exhausted me, and I fear I cannot keep up the fight for much longer. Do forgive me, Lindsey. The cultural education of your future wife must be abandoned.*

I hope this letter finds you well. Give my best to your dearest friend. Lady Pelham wishes me to pass along her regards for you both, and of course Emmeline's passion cannot be overstated.

Your loving sister,
Rowena

Lindsey glanced over to Aubrey. "What news from Emmeline?"

A pink tinge came to the tips of Aubrey's ears. "She's enjoying Paris very much. Gathered a few new ideas for electrifying the mill." He held out some of the papers in his hand—for Lindsey now realised Emmeline had stuffed many pages into the single envelope—and in doing so revealed far more diagrams than prose. "And sends her best to you, of course."

Lindsey chuckled.

Aubrey joined him, then trailed off with a thoughtful expression. "You haven't told them about the riding accident, have you?"

Nothing in Aubrey's tone bespoke the least interrogative intention, yet Lindsey's own guilt resounded regardless. "I'm afraid I haven't yet. I wanted to wait until…"

"Until you knew the final outcome?" Aubrey suggested.

"Until I could reassure them of your full recovery," Lindsey corrected, gentle yet firm. Though the obverse result had run through his mind over and over again throughout Aubrey's fever, now that his Aubrey was safe, he couldn't bring himself to even begin to think of the possibility. "I must confess myself more than happy to deliver them the good news."

Aubrey laid down the papers and reached out his hand. Lindsey took it without a second thought. Aubrey brought their clasped hands to his lips and kissed their interlaced fingers.

"Halloway told me he's nearly done with his painting," Aubrey said, gazing idly down at his own fingers tracing Lindsey's palm, as if unaware how thoroughly he'd melted Lindsey's heart just a moment prior. "Says he's just got the face left. Do you suppose he could capture my portrait from my bedside?"

Lindsey blinked, a little stunned by the sudden change in topic. "I suppose he could."

Aubrey's contented smile usually banished all possible concern from Lindsey's mind. And yet, even as he made a game attempt at returning the smile, his thoughts ran on. Unaccountably so, in his opinion. What did it concern him, that Aubrey would model for Halloway from his sickbed? Aubrey need do no more than lie supine, which he would do already, and would continue to do for as long as Dr Pilkington prescribed bed-rest. Since Halloway only required Aubrey's face, Aubrey's body would remain safe and snug beneath layer upon layer of bedclothes and blankets. There wasn't anything worrisome about the matter—never mind how badly the last modelling session had ended.

"By the time he's done with it," Aubrey said, startling Lindsey out of his troublesome thoughts, "I might be well enough to return to the stables."

"Return to the stables?" Lindsey interjected in a voice not quite under his own control.

The bewilderment which had vexed Lindsey these past few moments now appeared on Aubrey's face. "Yes. Get back on the horse, as the saying goes. In this case literally."

Lindsey, his throat tight, replied, "I'm not sure that's a good idea."

"Why not?" Aubrey's brow furrowed in confusion, total bewilderment in his tone.

Lindsey didn't have an answer. He had only his useless hands clenching his own knees. Then Aubrey's fingertips alighted upon his wrist. The tender warmth of them gave him strength enough to meet his gaze again.

"I'm not afraid," Aubrey began. "I want to build upon what I've already learnt, before I forget it all."

"I cannot in good conscience condone it," said Lindsey.

Aubrey's soft brown eyes flew wide at his firm tone.

"You nearly died," Lindsey continued, his voice not quite under his own control. "You've barely survived as it is. And when I recall that I am responsible for introducing you to the means of your own destruction—!"

"Lindsey," said Aubrey.

"You cannot deny this," Lindsey countered. "I suggested you take up horseback riding. Over your own protests, I encouraged you in its pursuit—"

"Lindsey," Aubrey said again.

"Purely for my own satisfaction!" Lindsey continued. "For my own selfish sake, I put you in such danger—!"

"Lindsey," Aubrey said a third time, and put a hand on Lindsey's shoulder for good measure.

Touch stopped Lindsey's tongue where mere words could not. He shut his mouth and gazed down upon Aubrey with a pleading expression.

"I want to learn to ride," Aubrey said, gazing seriously up into Lindsey's face with his dark and beautiful eyes. "Just as much as you wanted me to learn. I made the decision to try, with full knowledge of the associated risks. And I refuse to let you martyr yourself for my own folly."

"You've broken three ribs!" Lindsey protested.

"Cracked," Aubrey corrected him. "And we both know I've already survived far worse."

If Aubrey intended this assertion to calm Lindsey, he had erred. The recollection of what had befallen Aubrey in the Rook Mill boiler explosion served only to heighten Lindsey's dismay.

"When you came home from hospital," Lindsey began, then stopped himself. "No, I must go further back. When the explosion at Rook Mill occurred, and you were wounded in it—I couldn't go to you. It wasn't safe for either of us. But still I felt... All I wanted was to be with you. To hold you. To keep you safe and make you well. To know you were alive, and if your condition took a turn for the worse, to be beside you as you…"

Lindsey broke off, his words choked by a raw lump in his throat as tears came unbidden to his eyes. He raised his gaze to the ceiling and blinked furiously to keep them at bay. His breaths came ragged—he felt that if he opened his mouth again, he'd be helpless to hold back a sob, or worse—yet there remained so much more for him to say. With considerable force of will, he steadied himself and continued.

"I wasn't there for you. And I couldn't bear the thought of you suffering alone. I couldn't bear the thought of you suffering at all. And yet, we remained apart, for both our sakes, until you came home from hospital." Lindsey's eyes yet burned; he screwed them shut. "I cannot express the relief I felt—the joy I had—to hold you again. To know you were safe. To be with you once more."

With his eyes shut, he couldn't see Aubrey's face, couldn't trace through expression how his words were taken, what effect they had upon the listener. He forced them open. A scalding-hot tear fell down his cheek. He kept them open regardless, needed to see.

Aubrey gazed upon him with an expression of perfect bewilderment—and no small amount of concern. His pale brow furrowed, his lips parted, his wide eyes reflecting Lindsey's misery back upon himself.

Lindsey struggled to conclude his argument. "I was so happy to have you once again. But even then—I never saw your wounds. Never undressed them. Never witnessed what the explosion had done, not really."

"Because I wouldn't let you," Aubrey replied, his words dulled.

"No—I mean, yes, strictly speaking, you wouldn't, but—" Lindsey fought for the words required to make his point. "I've seen your scars. But I've never seen your injuries. I never saw you freshly wounded… until now."

A spark of comprehension lit Aubrey's eyes, yet the concerned furrow remained upon his brow.

Lindsey hurried to speak on, lest he be interrupted. "It's not that I find fault with you for it—It's only that I find I haven't the strength to see—" He stopped himself, took a deep breath, and finally admitted what he himself had not realised until now. "It shocked me, to see your bruises. It worried me, to come upon you lying helpless on the ground in the storm. It frightened me," and here his voice cracked again, "to turn in the saddle and find you'd vanished from my side."

Aubrey said nothing. But his hand came up to caress Lindsey's cheek, and that said far more.

"And to think it might happen again—" Lindsey began.

"You ride out whenever the opportunity strikes," Aubrey reminded him, his voice gentle.

"I do," Lindsey admitted, "but—"

Aubrey stopped him with a look; earnest, intense, pleading. "Do you think I don't worry about you when you do?"

Lindsey balked. It had never once occurred to him that his own sporting activities were anything to worry about. "You've never mentioned it."

"No, I haven't," Aubrey concurred. "But I've worried all the same. Still, I trust you to know your limits and keep your head about you afield. And I know that if anything should go wrong, I'll look after you."

"I've always trusted you would," said Lindsey, which earned him a flash of a half-smile from Aubrey.

"I'm not so worried about myself now," Aubrey continued. "Because I know I've got you. You might trust yourself to look after me. I think you've proved yourself more than capable thus far."

Then Aubrey smiled up at him; his rare, shy smile, raw and brilliant despite its hesitance.

Tears flooded Lindsey's eyes, blurred his vision, robbed him of the sweetest sight in all the world. Unable to bear it a moment longer, he embraced him, and Aubrey's return kiss did much to soothe his fearful heart.

~

The revelation of Lindsey's fears alarmed Aubrey. And yet, as sorry as he felt to cause Lindsey pain, he couldn't help how it warmed his heart to know the depths of Lindsey's concern. He channelled the overwhelming force of his sorrow and gratitude into his embrace, wishing he could do more to soothe the worried furrows in Lindsey's brow. Soon, the very moment he felt able, he would show Lindsey just how much he appreciated his tenderness and care. For now, he had strength only to clasp his arms around him and hold him tight.

The next few nights passed in quiet comfort. Morphine tablets numbed the stabbing pain of his cracked ribs and subdued his cough. Better medicine yet, by Aubrey's estimation, was the simple joy of Lindsey sleeping beside him, the warmth of his body beneath the sheets, and the familiarity of his long limbs curled around him.

By day, Aubrey continued to rest, though he spent more and more hours waking as the week went by. Lindsey remained beside him for much of it, answering correspondence from a writing-desk on his lap and reading books old and new, to himself as Aubrey slept, and aloud whenever he woke. They took breakfast and dinner together in Aubrey's sickroom. Lindsey spent luncheon with Halloway, at Aubrey's urging—it wouldn't do to neglect their friend. The afternoons, again at Aubrey's suggestion, he spent riding or otherwise out-of-doors. Aubrey couldn't bear to see Lindsey grow as pale and wan as himself, or deny him the opportunity to enjoy a truly splendid summer.

Whenever Lindsey went out, Halloway came in to draw Aubrey.

Portraiture modelling proved both easier and more difficult than the full-bodied business. Easier, in that he didn't have to keep the whole of his body as still as the grave, nor did he have to bare it to eyes and draughts alike. More difficult, in that both eyes and mouth had to remain fixed in place—eyes open and mouth closed for the miniature; mouth open and eyes shut for *Icarus Fallen*—which meant he could neither read nor converse to take his mind off the boredom of his sick-bed.

Had the artist been any man but Halloway, Aubrey would have perished of sheer monotony. But Halloway's amicable nature went a long way towards keeping Aubrey amused as he modelled. He knew a hundred dreadful stories from all the parties he and Graves attended: tales of wicked conversational sniping between dowager aunts and ne'er-do-well nephews, elderly confirmed bachelors and youthful braggarts, headstrong American heiresses and their more stoic but no less battle-ready English counterparts. Aubrey's real struggle soon became keeping a straight face as Halloway told enough humorous anecdotes to make himself hoarse by the end of the day's work.

All the legends of London set the wheels of Aubrey's mind

turning despite the opiate fog, and when a convenient break occurred in their work—Halloway setting aside his sketchbook to flex his fingers and allow Aubrey to stretch his neck—Aubrey took the opportunity to ask a singular question.

"Halloway," Aubrey said, "why do you live in Manchester?"

Halloway paused in his stretching. "Pardon?"

"Your gallery is in London," Aubrey said. "Most artists seem to be. And Graves is there as well. Why do you live in Manchester instead?"

"Don't suppose you'd believe me if I told you it was the light?" Halloway replied with a weak chuckle.

Aubrey gave him a blank look. The smog that covered Manchester hardly allowed for breathing, much less sunlight. Though he supposed London was much the same in that regard. "Why not the country, then?"

"The country is expensive," said Halloway. "Manchester is cheap—relatively speaking."

"Is that it?"

Halloway's moustache twisted to one side. "I suppose it is it... but it's not all, and I think all is what you're asking after." He hesitated, then retrieved his sketchbook from beneath the chair. Wordlessly, he flipped it open to a particular page, then handed it over to Aubrey.

Aubrey took the sketchbook, his mind afire with curiosity. His eyes fell upon a page dark with ink, splattered and scratched all over the parchment with fevered intensity, creating an image as heavy as what it depicted; the furnace of a steam engine, stoked by a half-dozen workmen, each bare to the waist. Their muscles rippled beneath Halloway's cross-hatching. Sweat dripped from their flesh, carving reserves of white through the stippled black soot. Aubrey could almost feel the heat of fire and man alike leaping off the page.

Halloway reached over and turned it.

Another scene of working men, this time constructing a railway, swinging sledge-hammers overhead to slam down upon iron railroad ties. Again their raw masculinity felt palpable, the taste of iron coming unbidden to Aubrey's tongue.

Aubrey turned the next page on his own, revealing a smelter in the steelworks; a navvy climbing scaffolding on the next; and on the page opposite that, a farrier shoeing a horse standing ready by a cart hauling bars of steel.

"These are magnificent," Aubrey said.

A wan smile flickered across Halloway's face. "That's how I knew."

What he knew need not be spoken of aloud. It was what all men like themselves knew of their own souls. Halloway had perceived the passion and beauty of working men, and in doing so, discovered something about himself.

"But," Halloway added, gently taking the sketchbook from Aubrey's hands, "it is not the sort of subject that sells in London. And London, as you yourself have said, is where all art is bought. It's where the money lives—at least, in the season."

Aubrey contemplated this new insight. "The money prefers Icarus?"

"Classical scenes in general," Halloway admitted. "And I must confess myself interested in those, as well. Very interested," he interjected with a suggestive cant of his eyebrows. "But I cannot deny a certain affinity for less fashionable subjects. And if I cannot sell them, I can at least hoard them for myself." He leaned in to add in a conspiratorial whisper, "And for Graves, as well. But good luck getting him to admit it."

Aubrey chuckled, though he felt surprised to learn that the Aesthete valued such things.

Dr Pilkington returned at the end of the week to check Aubrey's progress. His examination concluded Aubrey had recovered well, and could—finally—venture beyond the sickroom. The moment the doctor departed, Lindsey helped Aubrey to dress, then supported him on his arm as together they made their way downstairs to the makeshift studio in the ballroom.

While Halloway had spent afternoons capturing Aubrey's visage, he'd spent the following mornings transferring this image to the final painting. As such, when Aubrey at last descended, he gazed upon a nearly completed work.

"Fantastic!" Lindsey declared.

"You're too kind," Halloway replied with a coy smile.

Aubrey, meanwhile, had lost all power of speech. He'd never seen the like of the painting before in all his days. Not only due to its mythological setting and subject, nor to Halloway's undeniable talent. But for another reason entirely.

No one in Aubrey's life had ever before captured his likeness.

They had admired it and expressed a wish to possess it forever, but none had taken the plunge of preserving it. Until now.

Now, Aubrey gazed upon something he would be otherwise quite unable to see. While he might see his own face in the mirror each morning—whether he wanted to or not—he could never know how he appeared without locking gazes with his own reflection. In the mirror, and thus, in his mind's eye, there remained always a confrontational element, of those large dark eyes fixing upon him, no matter how he turned his head. His own defiance stared him down whenever he shaved his cheeks or combed his hair.

Icarus Fallen, however, showed him with his eyes shut.

For the first time in his life, Aubrey saw himself without defiance, without confrontation, without aggression. With his eyes shut, he saw soft lashes, a smooth brow, and a mouth whose curves no longer twisted in disgust at the burn scars sweeping alongside.

Aubrey saw the face Lindsey must have seen on the pillow next to him.

"Here," came Lindsey's gentle voice in his ear at that very moment.

Lindsey's grip shifted on his arm, giving the merest suggestion that he ought to turn. Aubrey glanced up at him first, then followed his gaze over his own shoulder, where Lindsey's other arm had pulled close the dining-room chair.

It occurred to Aubrey he must have stood staring at the painting for a very long and silent moment, for Lindsey to take such pains. Heat rushed to his cheeks. He looked up to Lindsey again and swallowed down his instinctive apology to say, instead, what he really meant. "Thank you."

Lindsey smiled and helped Aubrey down into the seat, afterwards laying his soft hand upon Aubrey's shoulder. Aubrey reached up to clasp that hand, and together they returned their gazes to the painting.

"How do you find it, then?" Halloway asked—for he of course remained, gazing upon his own handiwork with the same intensity as the others.

"It's..." Aubrey struggled to find a form of expression that wouldn't sound like mere flattery of himself as the painting's subject. "I've never seen its like."

The moment he said it, it occurred to him such commentary could be taken as a veiled insult.

But as he glanced at Halloway to see his reaction, he found his moustache curled in a grin.

"I wonder, then," Halloway said, stepping away from the painting and reaching for something else amongst his sketchbooks and brushes, "what you might think of this?"

So saying, he slipped a scrap of parchment into Aubrey's hand.

Aubrey glanced down and discovered, once again, his own face. This, then, was the miniature he'd commissioned, rendered in watercolours. Unlike *Icarus Fallen*, it depicted him with his eyes open. And yet the miniature's gaze, too, lacked the confrontational air Aubrey had come to expect from himself. He knew not how Halloway had done it, but he had somehow softened the eyes, and brought the barest hint of a smile to the lips. Aubrey felt his own face mirror the miniature's and recognised it as the expression he most often turned upon Lindsey.

Lindsey, meanwhile, had peered over Aubrey's shoulder. "By Jove!"

His exclamation came in a gasp, astonished into breathless quietude, yet it echoed through Aubrey's heart as if shouted.

Aubrey couldn't help grinning as he handed the miniature off to Lindsey, who took it with all the reverence of a pilgrim presented with a relic. Delight sparkled in his sapphire-blue eyes, and the smile Aubrey loved so dear spread over his lips.

"It's only half-done," Halloway explained over them. He'd shoved his hands into his trouser pockets and rocked on the balls of his feet like a schoolboy with a splendid secret. "Still need a matching one of you, Althorp. When you've a moment to sit for it."

"Of course!" said Lindsey, never taking his eyes off the miniature.

~

CHAPTER NINE

Dr Pilkington returned at the end of the week to check on Aubrey's progress. After a brief examination, he declared his patient well on the road to recovery—with a few caveats. While a short stroll through the garden at a leisurely pace would do Aubrey more good than harm, Dr Pilkington could under no circumstances permit any great exercise. A return to horseback-riding was right out.

Shortly after the doctor's departure, Charles informed Lindsey that the coachman, begging his pardon, would appreciate his opinion upon the acquisition of the blue roan yearling they'd spoken of earlier, at his leisure.

"Have him meet me in the library," said Lindsey.

"Or," Aubrey interjected, "we might go to see him in the stables."

Lindsey gave him a look which suggested he thought Aubrey must not have heard Dr Pilkington's prescription, then glanced at Charles. "I'll have a reply for him in a moment."

No sooner had the door clicked shut upon Charles's retreat than Lindsey turned to Aubrey again.

"I've been stuck indoors for weeks," said Aubrey in response to Lindsey's unspoken disbelief. "Light exercise would do me better than no exercise at all."

"Why don't we go for a walk in the gardens instead?" said Lindsey. "Perfectly unobjectionable, the gardens. And in bloom, no less."

"While I appreciate the compromise," Aubrey said, unable to suppress a fond smile even as he argued his point, "I don't think it will do me any harm to merely stand near a horse. I promise I won't attempt to mount any stallions. Present company excluded, of course."

Lindsey blinked at him, then snorted, turning away with a hand over his mouth to stifle the rest of his laughter.

Humour won out, and within the hour, Aubrey, supported on Lindsey's arm, took his first step outside in almost a month. Though every breath gave him a stinging reminder of his cracked ribs, he relished the taste of fresh air.

Upon their arrival at the stables, Aubrey relinquished his hold on Lindsey so the latter might more effectively converse with the coachman. Their talk of conformation and breeding didn't quite hold Aubrey's attention—for which he would later blame the morphine tablets—and he found himself wandering off down the interior of the stables, enjoying the warm atmosphere and the peculiar yet comforting scent of horses. At the opposite end from Lindsey and the coachmen, he encountered a familiar long face.

"Parsival," said Aubrey, halting his wanderings to address the gelding.

Parsival flicked one ear in his direction.

Aubrey considered the horse. He looked well, he thought. Certainly less damaged by their mutual misadventure than Aubrey himself.

"Sir?"

Aubrey, startled out of his musings, turned to find Fletcher had approached him in the meanwhile. Lindsey and the coachman were nowhere in sight, having evidently gone out of the stable altogether in the course of their conversation. Fletcher seemed as surprised to see Aubrey as Aubrey felt to see him.

"Good morning," Aubrey managed after a too-long pause.

Fletcher touched the brim of his cap in reply. "Is there anything I might help you with?"

The morphine tablets suppressed Aubrey's instinctive desire to admit to no need of assistance and scuttle away before he could make a greater fool of himself. Instead, he considered Fletcher's question at face value.

"Perhaps it's overly fanciful on my part," Aubrey said. "But I should like, if possible, to let him know that there are no hard feelings between us. I know it's not his fault I fell off. And it's not his fault the storm frightened him so." He looked self-consciously at Parsival, finding the gelding's soft brown gaze much easier to meet than the groom's bewildered stare. "I'd like to get to know him better, before I get back in the saddle. If that sounds like a reasonable goal. I wouldn't know. I've not much horse sense, as I'm sure you've noticed."

The last self-deprecating addition might have been better left in his head, but it was out now, and Aubrey dared a glance back at Fletcher's face to see how the groom took it.

While Aubrey wasn't watching, Fletcher's confusion had evidently turned to consideration. He looked Aubrey over for a moment longer before saying, "You might know him better afore your ribs heal up, but it'll take him much longer than that to know you. Nothin' personal," he added in response to some uncontrolled change in Aubrey's face. "They don't track time quite the same way we do. Don't trust near as easily."

"How long do you estimate it would take?" Aubrey asked.

"A year," Fletcher declared, though not without some semblance of regret in his eyes, as if he were sorry to be the one to crush any hopes. "Year an' a half, maybe."

Aubrey looked to Parsival again. He knew the gelding understood nothing of their conversation—only that two of the loud bipedal things, one familiar and one strange, had decided to make noise together in front of his stall. Still, Aubrey couldn't help projecting some small amount of anthropomorphism into the way Parsival bobbed his head and snorted.

Aubrey turned back to Fletcher and said, "No time like the present to get started."

"Then," said Fletcher, "you might want to start with this."

So saying, he produced a carrot from his trouser pocket and broke off a bite-sized chunk, which he held out to Aubrey. Aubrey took it, all the while very aware of Parsival's increased interest in him. The gelding's ears, which had 'til now swivelled idly atop his head, fixed themselves in Aubrey's direction, and his long neck stretched out of his stall to bring his nose to Aubrey's chest.

"Hold it out in your palm and keep your hand flat," Fletcher advised. "His teeth don't know the difference between a carrot and your fingers."

With renewed trepidation, Aubrey did as Fletcher instructed. No sooner had he made the carrot available to Parsival than the great flapping lips descended upon his hand to gobble up the treat. Parsival turned away as he munched, or so Aubrey thought, until he realised the turning of the enormous head had served to bring him fully into the focus of one deep brown eye.

"Put a hand on his neck," Fletcher suggested. "Gentle, now."

Aubrey carefully laid his horse-spit-slicked palm against Parsival's thickly muscled neck. He found it warm to the touch, soothingly so, and the short hair more like velvet than the bristle-board he'd expected. He gave Parsival a few soft, slow strokes, then dared to take his eyes off the gelding and turned back to Fletcher.

Fletcher's moustache twitched. "That wasn't so bad now, was it, sir?"

"No," Aubrey admitted, withholding a smile much like the one he suspected Fletcher had just suppressed. He continued petting Parsival all the while, the motion taking the edge off of his anxieties and allowing his mind to run down more productive paths. "What now? Aside from riding—I'm afraid doctor's orders have forbidden me from vaulting into the saddle again quite so soon."

Fletcher raised his brows. "There's not much else to a horse, sir. They like to eat, and they like bein' turned out to pasture. Only thing left for us to do is groom 'em, and broadly speakin', that's not considered fit work for a gen'leman such as yourself."

Aubrey's hand stopped mid-stroke upon Parsival's neck. He hadn't realised the staff thought of him as a gentleman. He certainly didn't think of himself as such, despite his constant efforts at maintaining his decorum. Decency, he thought he'd managed, but no workhouse brat ever grew up to be a gentleman, outside of a Dickens novel.

"If you think me unfit for such work," Aubrey began, choosing his words with care, "then I'll defer to your expertise. But I'm eager to learn, if you'll permit it."

He knew as well as any working man how obnoxious it could be when laypersons—particularly those in a position of power over one's self—took too keen an interest in one's trade. And while, on paper, Aubrey was as much Lindsey's employee as Fletcher was, it was plain Fletcher didn't see him that way. Fletcher might feel obligated to humour Aubrey no matter how outlandish his requests or how his presence interfered with the running of the stables.

Aubrey didn't want to make a nuisance of himself. And yet, he did sincerely wish to learn more of horse sense.

Fletcher gave him a considering look. "I don't suppose I see any objection. So long as it wouldn't injure your health."

Aubrey understood his concern. It wouldn't do to get the master's particular friend killed. "I promise I won't do anything beyond my strength."

He held out his hand to seal the bargain. After a moment, Fletcher clasped it warmly. Then he grabbed a fistful of fresh hay, twisted it into a sort of hand-broom, and began showing Aubrey how to whisk the dust from Parsival's coat. At last, Aubrey learnt the meaning of the word "withers" when Fletcher pointed to the beast's shoulders and informed him it was the safest place to stand near a horse, and the point from which he ought to begin brushing.

"Going with the grain of the hair, mind," Fletcher added as he handed the makeshift brush off to Aubrey.

Aubrey did as instructed. Parsival seemed to notice the change in hands, bending his massive neck to bring his head around to look at Aubrey. Aubrey stopped, and Parsival turned back, only to turn around again the moment Aubrey resumed. As Parsival's mouth inched closer to his shoulder, Aubrey looked to Fletcher for an answer.

"They groom each other in the pasture," Fletcher explained, leaning against a post as he watched the proceedings. "He's trying to return the favour. Though if you don't want him chewing your sleeve, just pat his neck and he'll settle down."

Aubrey reached out his hand accordingly, laying trembling fingers along the thick corded muscles, and Parsival let him alone. Aubrey continued brushing in silence. The repetitive nature of the work proved soothing in a manner he hadn't anticipated. He even forgot the watchful gaze of Fletcher, recalling his presence only when the groom spoke.

"May I be frank with you, sir?"

"By all means," Aubrey replied, and in doing so, thought he might be the first man in English history to speak the phrase in earnest.

Fletcher picked up a stalk of hay and twisted it between his thumb and forefinger. "I can't speak for everyone on the staff, but I think I speak for a good many of us when I say your arrival came as something of a relief."

Of all the things Aubrey might have anticipated hearing, this had certainly never occurred to him. He could do little more than blink in bewilderment.

"Before you arrived," Fletcher continued, "we were all rather in the expectation of one of us having to fill the post, as it were. Some fellows, I'm ashamed to say, took bets on who amongst us would have to do it. Some looked forward to it more'n others."

Aubrey stared in horror as he heard all his worst assumptions confirmed. In taking his place at Lindsey's side, he taken the place of some other man who aspired to advance his position—and, indeed, had been hired on for that purpose.

Fletcher shrugged. "Can't say I'd've minded it, but I always considered myself a groom first, and whatever else may come after that, second. Still—we were all on tenterhooks waitin' to see who the master might have. Made things more'n a little tense, as you might imagine. And then you come up like a dark horse. Everythin' relaxed after that. No more waitin' and wonderin' about what further duties might befall us. We could all get back to the business we were hired for—myself eagerly so. I like workin' with horses. You might've noticed," he added dryly.

Aubrey chuckled at that. Privately, he supposed it must prove much easier to concentrate on such work when one no longer had to keep an eye over one's shoulder in case today might be the day upon which one's master took particular notice of one's backside.

"What I'm tryin' to say, sir," Fletcher continued, "is we're glad to have you. You've made Sir Lindsey quite happy, and we'd like the household to continue on in such harmony as you've brought to it."

Words couldn't express the relief Aubrey felt to know the few voices he'd overheard didn't speak for all who worked upon the Wiltshire estate. He tried to convey a fraction of his immense gratitude in his reply. "Thank you, Fletcher."

Fletcher's moustache twitched in a smile.

He might have said more, but at that moment, the coachman returned to the stable with Lindsey.

Lindsey, mid-sentence—indeed, mid-word—broke off his conversation to stare at Aubrey.

Aubrey, still brushing Parsival, stared back. "Good morning."

"Good morning," Lindsey replied, appearing no less puzzled, though he nonetheless went back to speaking with the coachman, and only when he'd concluded their discussion of horseflesh did he turn his attention to Aubrey again.

Fletcher, meanwhile, had stepped forward to take the makeshift brush from Aubrey and untwist it back into mere hay, which then joined its brethren upon the floor of the stable, as though it'd never been anything more. Then, with another touch of his cap brim, Fletcher dismissed himself to continue his duties.

Aubrey resumed patting Parsival's neck as Lindsey approached. In response to the unspoken question writ large over Lindsey's features, he replied, "I promised I wouldn't ride a horse. I never said anything about grooming one."

Lindsey shook his head, chuckling. Then he offered Aubrey his arm once more and led him back up to the house.

~

Halloway took his leave on an unassuming morning in the middle of the week, just after breakfast. Aubrey and Lindsey bid him farewell in the library and watched through the window as the family carriage rattled off down the drive to deliver Halloway to the train station, and from thence to London, where he would reunite with Graves and give over his masterpiece to the gallery.

Some hours passed in quiet recreation, with Lindsey perusing the *Strand*, Aubrey the *Engineer*. The crunch of wheels on gravel announced the return of the family carriage. Aubrey glanced up in idle curiosity, intending to resume his reading in short order, but found his attention arrested by the sight in the courtyard.

"Emmeline?" he blurted in disbelief.

"What?" said Lindsey, looking up from his own literature.

"Emmeline," Aubrey repeated—for the woman who alighted from the carriage wore a brilliant chartreuse gown that could belong only to her. Another woman followed in a dress of more sedate robin's egg blue, setting off the golden gleam of hair curling from beneath her hat. "And Rowena."

"By Jove!" said Lindsey, who'd gone to the window to confirm Aubrey's report. "Suppose they've had their fill of Paris?"

They hadn't long to wonder, for Emmeline appeared as little more than a streak of chartreuse as she hurried into the house, and soon afterwards she appeared in the library doorway, her hat askew and her cheeks flushed pink.

"Aubrey!" Emmeline cried.

This was all the warning he received before she swooped down upon him.

Aubrey braced himself for the impending crush, but his preemptive wince appeared to warn her off, and the embrace she gave him proved none so tight as he'd feared from her urgency. Her delicate arms wound around his shoulders as gentle as butterfly wings, though the brim of her hat flattened against his face. He tucked it out of the way as gingerly as he could manage from his disadvantaged position, then returned her embrace as softly as she'd given it. At length, she released him.

"Are you quite well?" she asked, laying the back of her hand against his forehead as if by instinct, then snatching it away as she realised what she'd done.

"Well on the mend," Aubrey assured her, unable to suppress his own fond smile at her evident concern.

Rowena, meanwhile, had entered the library, having followed her friend at a more sedate pace. She turned to her brother, still standing at the window.

"We had a letter," Rowena explained, "saying the chief electrical engineer had fallen off a horse and caught pneumonia."

"So of course," Emmeline interrupted, "we couldn't possibly delay our return another moment! We simply had to see you—and to render whatever assistance we might!"

"We passed Mr Halloway at the train station," Rowena continued speaking to her brother with perfect *sangfroid*. "Most convenient, for then we didn't have to send for the carriage. I believe another quarter-hour's wait would have killed her."

"Happy, then," Lindsey replied, enough recovered from Emmeline's ambush to join the conversation, "that coincidence prevented her from leaving me a widower."

"But how are you, really?" Emmeline urged, still intent upon Aubrey.

"I'm quite all right, now," said Aubrey.

"Three broken ribs," Lindsey cut in.

"Cracked," Aubrey countered. "Not broken."

"And not yet healed, either," Lindsey reminded him, putting his hands on the back of Aubrey's chair.

Aubrey wished he'd focus more on the positive aspects of his recovery. "I've thrown off the pneumonia, at least."

"And thank goodness for that!" Emmeline chimed in.

"I'd thought you'd find it a disappointment," said Rowena, not bothering to feign surprise. "You seemed so intent upon nursing him. Alas, we've arrived too late."

"I did get to use oxygen canisters," Aubrey offered.

Emmeline's expression brightened. In wondrous hushed tones, she asked, "Did you, indeed?"

Behind her back, Rowena rolled her eyes and beckoned her brother closer to form their own conversation.

Aubrey ignored her in favour of divulging all the details of the oxygen canisters to Emmeline's evident delight. She in turn told him all the technical splendour of Eiffel's tower.

And yet, even as he fell back into familiar discourse, there remained a disquieting notion in the back of his mind that, before the end of their visit, he had best speak to the other lady returned to the house this day.

The opportunity to do so did not arise until after dinner. Having returned to the library, Aubrey witnessed Rowena tap Lindsey on the shoulder and whisper a few choice words into his ear. Aubrey could not actually discern which words she used, but he concluded they had something to do with the duties of a gentleman towards his bride-to-be, because no sooner had she spoken them than Lindsey took Emmeline aside and engaged her in conversation regarding her experiences at the House of Worth. Rowena herself retreated to a settee, and before she could open *Belgravia*, Aubrey took the chance to approach her.

"Rowena," Aubrey said with hesitance—despite the many months passed since she'd granted him permission, it still felt odd to address her by her Christian name. "I've some enquiries about the staff, and I'd hoped you might…"

"Serve as your fountain of knowledge?" she finished for him with a wry smile. "It would be my pleasure. What do you wish to know?"

"What are their names?"

She blinked at him, her wry smile frozen on her lips.

As the heat rose in his cheeks and ears, Aubrey hastened to add, "I know Charles, of course, and Mr Hudson—and Fletcher—and I've already been introduced to Miss Owen, but otherwise I'm afraid

I'm quite ignorant."

"Introduced," Rowena echoed, incredulous, "to Miss Owen?"

"Yes," Aubrey affirmed, despite his better instincts.

A single line appeared between Rowena's brows as she gazed upon him with an expression of utter bewilderment. "I'm sure I don't know who—Oh! Do you mean Freddie?"

Aubrey took on her confusion. "I…"

"Miss Winifred Owen," Rowena clarified. "Whom the other maids call Freddie."

"She is a housemaid, yes," said Aubrey, relieved to find a common understanding at last.

"Then I hardly see why you required an introduction," Rowena replied, half to herself. With a sly glance from under her lashes, she added, "Should I worry after your intentions for her?"

Aubrey, unamused, didn't see fit to answer her little jest. "No one else has told me her name, or the names of anyone working in the house. I had to ask it of her for myself. I'm willing to do the same for everyone else, if I must."

"But you had hoped I might have an easier answer for you," she concluded. "I do. I know the names of all the staff by heart. Such a feat is not typically expected of gentlemen, though I suppose you have your reasons for asking."

"I am unaccustomed," Aubrey said with forced calm, "to live amongst strangers."

"They're hardly strangers, Aubrey."

"Not to you, perhaps," Aubrey allowed. "You've hired them yourself. Or grown up with them. It's all rather different for me. I'm thrust into a sea of persons whom I mustn't acknowledge, yet who know all about me and my life as I lead it here. It's… unsettling. And I'd hoped if I knew something more of them—could recognise them on sight, at least—it might help things feel more settled."

He waited, with the horrible sensation of having divulged more than he'd intended, for whatever cutting remark she might use to dismiss his concerns.

Whatever levity she had prepared in response did not leave her parted lips, for realisation dawned upon her face and stopped her cold. The customary arch of her brows fell into a more natural expression. After a moment's hesitation, she replied in a low tone and with more warmth than before, "I see."

Aubrey waited.

After another moment's consideration, she added, "The best assistance I might provide, I believe, would come in the form of a written list, of all the staff, their duties, and a brief description of their appearance. I can have it ready for you by nightfall."

A fraction of the tension in Aubrey's chest melted into relief. "Thank you."

"You're quite welcome," she replied, and seemed about to say more, but something over Aubrey's shoulder caught her eye.

Aubrey turned to find Lindsey approaching and Emmeline vanished.

"What happened to your *fiancée?*" Rowena asked before he could speak a word.

"She's gone upstairs," Lindsey replied, blithe as ever, "to fetch her sketches of Eiffel's tower."

"Just as well, I suppose," said Rowena. "We were just speaking of the staff."

Lindsey's smile faded. He glanced between Aubrey and Rowena. In an instant, Aubrey knew precisely which mistaken assumption he had come to, and how, but even as he opened his mouth to correct it, he knew he would prove too late.

"I had meant to ask you about it," said Lindsey, despite Aubrey's silent screams for him to stop. "Though I didn't like to put it in writing, so I rather thought it might wait until you came home. Aubrey has already told you all the details of the incident, I presume."

Rowena stared at her brother. "What incident."

"It's hardly worth calling an incident," Aubrey protested, to no avail.

Lindsey cast a sympathetic look at him, yet continued speaking to his sister, as though Aubrey weren't pleading with everything short of words for him to shut his mouth on the subject. "Some of the staff have taken issue with Aubrey's presence in the house."

Aubrey wished for the cunning and craft required to surreptitiously strangle himself with his own necktie. Alas, he had no such skill.

"What happened, exactly?" Rowena pressed.

"I overheard a conversation," Aubrey cut in before Lindsey could say more, adding, with reluctance, "Two conversations. Whatever was said, it's my own fault for eavesdropping."

"And what," Rowena asked, turning her full attention upon him, "was said?"

Seeing no way out of it, Aubrey answered her, though it took considerable effort to force the words past his lips. "The maid who used to clean the master bedroom declared herself afraid of my face. Which is understandable. And before you ask, the issue is already resolved, for the other maid she spoke to readily agreed to trade rounds with her."

"This other maid is Freddie, I presume," said Rowena. "Or Miss Owen, as some know her."

"Yes," Aubrey admitted. He didn't dare look to Lindsey to see what he thought of the matter.

Rowena waited for him to continue, and when he did not, prompted, "And the other conversation?"

Aubrey pulled the words from his teeth like taffy. "A footman said he wished I might wear a bell, so they could all be warned of my coming and be spared the sight of my scars."

Rowena raised an eyebrow, which was about as much reaction as Aubrey would have expected of her.

Lindsey, however, defied expectations.

"What," he said, in a voice so low, so flat, and so cold as to immediately demand Aubrey's attention.

Aubrey glanced his way at last and found Lindsey looking quite unlike himself. He'd had a glimpse of it before, when he'd first told Lindsey of the incidents—all the angles of his face hardened, not even a hint of a smile to soften his sharp cheekbones or formidable brow, his blue eyes cold as ice without the warm sparkle of his sunny disposition.

Yet all Lindsey said when he unclenched his jaw to speak was, "Why didn't you tell me?"

"I did," Aubrey protested.

"You told me something had occurred, yes," Lindsey conceded, "but nothing of what was actually said."

Aubrey hated the tone Lindsey's voice had taken—a wavering note had come into its solemn timbre, a layer of hurt woven into its concern. He wished Lindsey would shout at him instead. He knew how to handle anger. "I didn't think it worth your while."

"Didn't think—?" Lindsey cut himself off, shaking his head and turning away.

"What difference does it make?" Aubrey asked.

"It makes every difference!" Lindsey cried, raising his voice at last as he whirled to face him again. "He said he wished to bell you like a cat!"

"Which is hardly the worst thing anyone's ever said of me," Aubrey insisted. "Sit down."

"I will when we have rid our household of whosoever possesses such a foolish tongue."

"That won't fix anything," said Aubrey, desperate to regain control over the conversation even as he felt it slipping away through his fingers, like the reins of a bolting horse.

"He's right," said Rowena.

These two words accomplished all Aubrey's protestations could not. Lindsey stopped talking, pacing, or gesturing, and instead focused all his energies upon serving a blank stare to his sister.

Rowena continued. "If Aubrey's first exercise of his authority as a member of our family is to weed out the staff's ranks, they may very well come to view him as something of a Robespierre, lopping the heads off all who give offence. And one can hardly blame them for it."

Aubrey hadn't words enough to express his gratitude for her adept assessment. Yet before he could even say so little as thank-you, Lindsey spoke.

"What, then," he urged, "would you have me do?"

"Nothing," said Rowena. "I'll have a word with Mr Hudson and Mrs Sheffield."

"No," said Lindsey.

Rowena looked as shocked as Aubrey felt.

"We cannot always await your return before resolving our domestic issues," Lindsey explained. "Particularly if we are to continue with setting up our own establishment in Manchester. You've said yourself that Emmeline, wonderful as she is, cannot be relied upon to resolve complaints amongst the staff. Therefore, in your absence, it must fall to me." He paused, then added, "Irregular as such an arrangement may be."

"There seems to be very little about our domestic arrangement which could be described as regular," Rowena noted dryly. "But I concede your point. What shall you do in my stead?"

Rather than answer his sister, Lindsey turned to Aubrey.

"Don't leave it up to me!" Aubrey protested before he could begin.

A hint of a smile returned to Lindsey's face at last. "As you wish. But neither do I intend to act without your approval. You must admit you are very much concerned in the matter."

"Not by choice," Aubrey muttered.

"We've already established," Lindsey went on, "that those who disparage you appear to be in the minority. This maid—Miss Owen—certainly does not dislike you. And I am convinced those in the stables hold you in regard."

Aubrey, recalling his conversation with Fletcher, cleared his throat. "I find them very good fellows."

Rowena's left eyebrow achieved an angle hitherto unprecedented. "And the footmen?"

At the reminder, Lindsey's face hardened again.

Glancing between the siblings and seeing no way through but the truth, Aubrey swallowed his pride and spoke. "Rowena, when you hired the footmen... I'm told they may have been selected in anticipation of certain other duties which might not befall them in other households."

Colour came to Lindsey's cheeks. He turned aside and coughed, no longer able to meet his sister's gaze.

"They were," Rowena replied without a trace of shame.

Aubrey plunged ahead. "I believe some among them might consider their hopes dashed by my arrival."

Lindsey's eyes went quite round. Apparently the possibility hadn't occurred to him. Warmth spread through Aubrey's heart at the reminder of Lindsey's good nature, unassuming and optimistic, never even considering the pettier aspects of humanity. Though even now he had to admit this charming naïveté might not serve them well in confronting the issue at hand.

Rowena, on the other hand, appeared nonplussed by this revelation. "And you fear these dashed hopes may have begotten the bitter feelings now expressed in idle gossip amongst them."

"Indeed," said Aubrey, relieved she'd grasped the issue so quickly.

She brought a hand to her chin. "It is certainly something to consider, moving forward."

Lindsey cleared his throat. "We can hardly accuse the staff of allowing jealousy to interfere with their duties."

"Not directly," Aubrey agreed. "But I think Rowena's suggestion—talking to Mr Hudson and Mrs Sheffield—is a good start."

Lindsey nodded. "I certainly shall."

And yet, as Aubrey considered the problem, he wondered if it would be sufficient. Lindsey talking to the butler and the housekeeper, they in turn passing the message along to the under-butler and cook, the footmen and maids, and then trickling out-of-doors to the grooms and sundry other persons Aubrey couldn't name but felt quite sure must exist to maintain the massive estate. A message which began strong enough from Lindsey's lips might dilute as it dispersed through the staff.

"Though I wonder," Lindsey added, as if reading Aubrey's thoughts, "if I might speak with the staff as a whole." In response to Rowena's alarmed expression, he added, "Not regarding the footman's jealousy, you understand. But regarding our expectations of their respect for Aubrey in general. I think the subject is worthy of direct address."

Rowena gave her assent just as Emmeline reappeared in the doorway, sketchbook in hand.

~

Lindsey had a great fondness for the Wiltshire house. The beautiful serenity of its grounds, the sport of its hounds and horses, and the fresh air all delighted him. But above all else, he had a particular love of falling asleep with his arms wrapped around his Aubrey and the low, comforting sounds of a country summer evening floating in through the open window.

Tonight, however, he found his gentle peace tainted by the knowledge that two of his own staff had said words against his Aubrey.

He knew, of course, as all gentlemen did, that staff would gossip about the family of whatever house they worked in. But he'd always assumed such gossip would limit itself to more harmless topics. Gossip about what a fool the master of the house was to buy a certain horse at such a price. Gossip about how he let his tender feelings, which shied away from the culling of runts, prevent the hound-master from maintaining an efficient pack. Gossip about his taste in clothes, or his eating habits, or which periodicals he had delivered to which house, and which ones went unread, and which ones fell apart with reading.

But gossip regarding his Aubrey...

Lindsey didn't consider himself a temperamental man, but the thought was enough to make his pulse pound. This pounding pulse kept him awake well after Aubrey had fallen asleep beside him. The sight of Aubrey's face in sleep—all furrows of concern smoothed from his brow, no worry curling the corners of his lips, his heavy lids shut over his soulful eyes, and his narrow chest slowly rising and falling in the steady breath of true repose—could only do so much to soothe him. For to look upon such a handsome face and know others thought it hideous stoked the furnace of his discontent.

He fell asleep at last, clasping Aubrey tight as if his arms could shield him from the slings and arrows of all the world. But upon waking, he did not find his irritation diminished. Not even Aubrey's kiss, an affectionate peck on his lips before they rose to dress, could banish it. He buried it deep beneath his affection for the man who shared his home, his bed, his life, but though he kept it hidden, it surged on.

The irritation lasted through breakfast and failed to diminish as Aubrey went off with Emmeline to renew their work upon the electrical conversions, and Rowena retired to her parlour to conduct her correspondence, and Lindsey summoned Mrs Sheffield and Mr Hudson to the library and asked them to assemble all the household staff in the foyer.

"Everyone, sir?" asked Mr Hudson.

Lindsey could hardly blame him for wanting clarification. It was, after all, an unprecedented command. Still, Lindsey gave no more explanation beyond a grim nod. "Everyone."

Mr Hudson bowed, Mrs Sheffield curtsied, and both departed. Lindsey waited in silent impatience, watched a quarter-hour tick past on the mantel clock, before Charles appeared upon the library threshold and announced the staff awaited him in readiness.

Lindsey crossed the house to the foyer, where he found the whole staff of the country house—some twenty-odd persons—standing shoulder-to-shoulder, stretched out across the bottom of the grand staircase. Mr Hudson, Mrs Sheffield, Fletcher and the other grooms from the stable, the hound-master, the gardener, the game-keeper, the cook, the maids in their tidy black-and-white uniforms, and the footmen in their livery. His gaze lingered upon the footmen in particular. One of these, he knew, had taken particular issue with Aubrey. He wished he could tell the wolf from the sheep. He wished he'd paid better attention to who worked for him, so he might know the man from description alone. He wished his sister had not been quite so thorough or so fashionable in her efforts to procure a well-matched set of male servants.

"Good morning, sir," said Mr Hudson.

Lindsey blinked, recalling where he stood and for what purpose. He smiled in appreciation for the gentle reminder, and returned, "Good morning."

There, his speech stuttered to a halt. The vast expanse of staff loomed before him—some loyal, some traitorous, and no way to tell one from another—in such numbers as to intimidate any would-be public speaker.

Lindsey cleared his throat and said the first thing that came into his head. "I suppose you're all wondering why I've gathered you here."

A score of blank stares turned upon him, which he supposed was as much as he deserved for such an opening. He swallowed and continued.

"First and foremost, allow me to extend my sincerest gratitude and appreciation. Your diligence, your honesty, and your loyalty are truly to be admired. For these, and for all the services you do for our family, I thank you."

This went over better than his first attempt. While none amongst his audience broke tradition to smile outright, many stood up straighter, shoulders shifting back and chins rising, taking more positive notice of his address.

Emboldened, Lindsey went on. "On this day, I would ask one further service of you."

Curiosity rippled through the crowd. Lindsey waited another moment to assure himself he held their full attention, then pressed on.

"From this moment forward, you are to consider Mr Warren as a member of the Althorp family."

Though he tried to restrain himself, his eyes wandered over towards the line of footmen as he added, "As much deserving of your respect, your diligence, and your loyalty as my sister, my *fiancée*, or myself."

The footmen appeared no less stoic than the rest of the staff, though Lindsey thought he caught a nervous swallow bobbing down the throat of one particular footman. Before his eyes spoke too much of his suspicions, Lindsey returned his gaze to the assembly as a whole.

"If you feel you cannot in good conscience do what I have asked, you may speak to Miss Althorp, and she shall find you a place in another household—a place as good or better than what you hold here, and with a letter of highest recommendation. I should be heartbroken to see any of you go, but I understand what I ask of you is not often asked in other households, and in those you may find yourself more comfortable."

Lindsey had gone over these particulars with Rowena the evening before, and together, they had decided upon this as the most amicable resolution. As he spoke the words now, he glanced over each face for any sign of dismay or outrage. He caught none— though he supposed if he were in their place, he too would endeavour to keep such feelings hidden from his employer.

"I have no wish to chide you," Lindsey continued, "or to cast judgment. I only ask that you continue to conduct yourselves with the same integrity I have come to know and appreciate from each and every one of you." He glanced over the gathering one final time, and as much to his own relief as theirs, finally concluded, "Thank you. That is all."

It was no St Crispin's Day, but it would suffice.

~

Aubrey waited in the breakfast room just off the foyer, listening to Lindsey's speech, arms crossed, chin tucked into his chest, brow furrowed in concentration. It followed all the same points as they'd laid out the night previous, yet still, to hear it in Lindsey's voice gave it new life. Resonant tones, equal parts mellifluous and heartfelt, granted a level of sincerity to his words which compelled the listener to attend. Aubrey only hoped the staff would see it in the same light.

The speech concluded, and the air filled with the echoes of scores of heels clicking against the marble floor as the staff returned to their posts. These echoes had not yet faded away before the door to the breakfast room opened and Lindsey entered. He seemed a little surprised to find Aubrey so near the door. Aubrey, meanwhile, noted the wan lines of his brow and the tight cast of his mouth.

"You heard it, then?" Lindsey asked.

"I did," said Aubrey. "If baronets served in the House of Lords, you might've made an adept member of Parliament."

A smile returned to Lindsey's lips at last, no less handsome for its bashful nature. "I've had my fill of speech-making, I think. Though they seemed to take it well enough."

Aubrey stepped up to slip his hands under Lindsey's jacket and wind his arms around his waist. "I prefer you at home, anyhow."

Lindsey bent to kiss him. When they broke off their embrace some moments later, Aubrey kept one hand upon Lindsey's lower back, unwilling to relinquish his hold entirely.

"I don't suppose," Lindsey said as they wandered out of the breakfast room and towards the library, "that I could induce you to give your opinion upon staffing the Manchester house?"

Aubrey hesitated. "I'd like to see what comes of your speech first."

Lindsey conceded the point with a nod.

Aubrey couldn't help feeling some small measure of relief at his dropping the subject. His fears regarding Miss Murphy and Miss Owen's reaction to Lindsey's speech, Aubrey kept to himself. Given what he knew of the two young women—little enough of the latter, and still less of the former—he considered his fears irrational. Still, they remained in the back of his mind, buzzing like trapped bees against his skull.

They'd reached the library by then, Lindsey settling into his armchair and picking up a nearby novel, no doubt discarded by his sister. Aubrey attempted to lose himself in *The Engineer*.

Little more than a half-hour later, Rowena entered the library.

"George has elected to seek his fortune outside of our establishment," she announced.

Lindsey glanced up from his book with a furrowed brow. "George?"

By way of explanation, she replied, "Cleft chin, small ears, blue eyes, brown hair with a slight curl."

Lindsey gave Aubrey an enquiring look.

Aubrey nodded in confirmation. As Rowena had spoken, the knot of anxiety in his chest had eased to know the footman who considered his face too ugly to be borne would no longer haunt the halls of their household.

Lindsey relaxed as well, smiling up at his sister. "Then it seems we may rest easy."

"And the rest of the staff?" Aubrey asked.

"No one else has yet come forward," said Rowena. "Have you given any further thought to whom among them you may bring to the Chorlton-cum-Hardy house?"

Again, Lindsey looked to Aubrey to provide an answer.

"Miss Murphy seems an adept cook, if she'll have us. And Miss Owen," Aubrey added. "Or Freddie, as you call her."

"You have then consigned yourself to the necessity of staff?" asked Rowena.

There was nothing teasing in her tone, yet Aubrey couldn't help reading something wry in her expression. "I have. Though I won't deny it's bizarre to always have at least one extra person in every room whom one must pretend isn't there."

A half-smile of amusement flickered across her lips. "In the interest of further dispelling the awkward nature of such an arrangement, perhaps you would like to join me in informing them of their good fortune?"

Aubrey knew as well as Lindsey that gentlemen taking personal interest in household management was not the done thing. Yet as Lindsey himself had just proved, the done thing was not necessarily done in their establishments. And while Rowena might very well smile at the notion, the smile she wore now bore more resemblance to her brother's natural ebullience than her usual dry wit. He concluded her offer was sincere. "I would, thank you."

Rowena turned to her brother. "Lindsey?"

For a third time, Lindsey glanced to Aubrey before making his reply. "I've done rather my fill of household management for the morning."

"Then," said Rowena, "I would ask you, Aubrey, to meet me in the morning room in a quarter-hour."

Aubrey nodded, and she swept out of the room.

"Unless you wanted me to go along?" asked Lindsey.

Aubrey smiled and shook his head. Lindsey returned to his book with an expression of some relief.

A quarter-hour later, Aubrey found his way to the morning room. There sat Rowena in her rose velvet armchair with the posture of an empress upon her throne.

"Perfectly punctual," she declared as Aubrey sat down beside her with considerably less grace or ease. "I do so admire that about you."

Aubrey hardly had time to thank her before the door opened again to reveal two maids in uniform on the threshold. He recognised one as Miss Owen. The other, a much taller and broader young woman with a square jaw, snub nose, and black curls escaping from beneath her white cap, he presumed to be Miss Murphy. Both curtsied upon the threshold.

"Good morning," said Rowena as they entered.

Miss Owen echoed the greeting in soft and muted tones. Miss Murphy offered it up as one accustomed to speaking clearly above the noise of clanging pots and pans in a busy kitchen.

"Do sit down." Rowena gestured broadly to the matched set of chairs before her.

Both maids did so, Miss Owen looking about as uncomfortable as Aubrey felt, with Miss Murphy at considerably more ease.

"Before we begin," said Rowena, "I would like to allay any concerns you may have. This is not a disciplinary meeting. This is an opportunity."

Miss Owen relaxed a fraction, bringing her head up along with her eyes.

"As you are no doubt well aware," Rowena continued, "Sir Lindsey requires a larger body of staff in Chorlton-cum-Hardy to prepare the household for his impending marriage. I believe you, Siobhan, have already volunteered to join this new establishment?" At Miss Murphy's eager nod, Rowena concluded, "Then Mr Warren and I have the happy privilege of informing you he and Sir Lindsey are quite satisfied with your performance as cook during this past season and look forward to your filling the post in Manchester."

Miss Murphy beamed. "Thank you, Miss Althorp!"

"And now we come to the position of housekeeper. Freddie," said Rowena, turning to Miss Owen. "Your people are yet in Wales, are they not?"

"Yes, miss," said Miss Owen.

"Would you be willing to live some further distance from them?"

Rowena asked. "With the addition of a pay raise, and the status of one in training to be a housekeeper in her own right?"

"I would, miss."

"Excellent." Rowena turned to Aubrey. "Have you any further enquiries, Mr Warren?"

He did, indeed. He'd spent the last hour ruminating upon them, and yet come no nearer to finding a phrasing fit for polite society. Still, he had to be sure. He cleared his throat. "Miss Murphy."

Rowena's left eyebrow twitched. Aubrey knew he'd erred in her eyes by not using Miss Murphy's Christian name. But in this moment, her opinion was not the one most important to him.

Miss Murphy herself took the solecism in stride, responding with a bright, "Yes, sir?"

"It's a pleasure to make your acquaintance at last. I've very much enjoyed your cooking these past months, and am glad for the opportunity to tell you so myself."

Dimples appeared in her cheeks as she smiled. "Thank you, sir."

"As you may not have had the opportunity to see me in person before his moment…" Aubrey turned his head to bring the scarred side into her full view, and gestured towards it with an open palm. "Does the sight of my face at all distress you?"

Her eyes widened, but apparently more at the audacity of his question than at his scars, for he'd made no effort to hide them from her before. "No, sir."

Rowena, too, had wide eyes, and one hand clenched the arm of her chair, but otherwise she made no sign she disapproved of Aubrey's line of questioning.

Aubrey smiled. "Thank you, Miss Murphy. Miss Owen," he continued, turning to her. "Though you and I have already met in passing, I must confess I wish to be absolutely sure before I force anyone to live in the company of such a gruesome sight. And so I ask, does my face distress you?"

Miss Owen showed no emotion as she replied, "No, sir."

"Thank you, Miss Owen," said Aubrey.

Rowena drew breath, as if to conclude this meeting before Aubrey could embarrass her further.

Miss Owen spoke first. "My brother has a similar look about him."

Miss Murphy and Rowena alike turned to look at her. Aubrey

found himself no less compelled.

This attention appeared to unsettle Miss Owen, but she nevertheless spoke on. "An explosion in the mines."

No wonder she had such familiarity with the oxygen canisters. Aubrey found his voice. "He has my sympathies."

"Thank you, sir," said Miss Owen. "He gets by all right."

His concerns satisfied, and with more to ruminate upon, Aubrey sat back and let Rowena resume control over the conversation. He half-listened as she informed the young ladies what they might expect from Manchester, and when she would send them on to assume their new roles, and what their new wages would be, and dismissed them. Miss Murphy and Miss Owen curtsied again and departed.

"Well!" said Rowena when they had gone, drawing Aubrey out of his thoughts. "I suppose if I ever find myself unable to hint at a point, I might call upon you to cut to the quick."

Aubrey bit back a smile. "I suppose you might."

~

The tailored waistline of the jacket drew the eye to his narrow hips. The buckskin breeches clung to his thighs, and the boots— particularly the stark and brilliant gleam of the polished black leather—displayed his shapely calves to their fullest.

"Well?" asked Aubrey.

Lindsey looked up into those beautiful brown eyes, and realised he'd spent perhaps a moment too long staring at the splendid sight of Aubrey in his new riding clothes. "It suits you."

Aubrey's brow furrowed in a manner suggesting he didn't quite believe him.

Lindsey crossed the room, gently plucked the black silk top hat from under Aubrey's arm, and laid it upon his head like a victory wreath.

"Your crowning glory," Lindsey announced, unable to help himself.

His indulgence was rewarded in a snort of laughter from Aubrey, who quickly covered it with a cough. Aubrey turned to pick up the final piece of his new ensemble—a pair of gloves—from where he'd laid them out on the bed whilst dressing. In doing so, he showed off, however unwittingly, the flattering effect of the buckskin breeches upon an already handsome behind.

"See something you like, then?"

Lindsey jerked his head up at the question and caught Aubrey's eye looking right back at him over his shoulder. No one could withstand the inquisition of such a sculpted ebony eyebrow as Aubrey cocked at Lindsey in that moment.

Warmth rushed to Lindsey's cheeks. "Rather, yes."

Aubrey rose laughing and turned to lead the way out of the room—pausing as he passed by to give Lindsey a kiss as light and fleeting as a snowflake.

Lindsey felt more than content to follow.

In the stables, Lindsey chose his steed with greater care than he had the afternoon of the accident. Atalanta, for all her speed, he now considered too hot-blooded and skittish for a ride in the country with his Aubrey. Fletcher suggested another gelding, called Galahad, as a fit match for Parsival, as the two horses' stalls stood side-by-side in the stables, and the animals had a bond not unlike friendship.

Once the grooms had both horses tacked up and led out to the stable yard, Lindsey again assisted Aubrey in mounting—for, while Dr Pilkington had declared his patient strong enough for exercise, said patient had spent so much time on bed rest as to lose some of his strength. However, with Lindsey's assistance, Aubrey vaulted up into the saddle on his first attempt, and, from his lofty seat, grinned down at Lindsey in thanks.

Lindsey mounted his own gelding at speed. A groom opened the gates, and they rode off side-by-side. Out of the corner of his eye, Lindsey watched Aubrey breathe deep of the fresh country air— breathe deep for the first time in weeks—and marvelled at how quickly he had attained such a fine seat, with supple waist and shoulders rolled back, combined with the riding jacket and breeches to make a splendid figure of him.

They rode on across fields and into woodland until they came upon a meadow fit for their picnic luncheon—cucumber sandwiches and muffins with jam. Having polished this off, Lindsey stripped down to his shirtsleeves, leaned back against the trunk of an accommodating oak, and found Aubrey leaning against him in turn. The warm weight of him thrilled through Lindsey's frame. He slung his arm around him, holding him snug, and Aubrey in turn raised his head to meet Lindsey's adoring look with his own affectionate gaze.

And the clouds, thank God, did not turn grey.

They returned to the stable yard just as the sun began to sink in the sky. Amongst the grooms, Fletcher looked particularly relieved to see the geldings returned without empty saddles. Having turned over their steeds, Lindsey and Aubrey went into the house and upstairs to their bedroom to change.

"What do you think of your second ride?" Lindsey asked him, bending to remove his own top-boots.

"I wouldn't say it's over quite yet," Aubrey remarked.

Lindsey gave him a quizzical glance and found his deep brown eyes sparkling with mischief. This was all the warning he received before Aubrey captured his mouth in a kiss.

More than willing to be thus entangled, Lindsey let Aubrey guide him back towards the bed. Two pairs of hands undid buttons and ties all the while, jackets and waistcoats dropping to the floor in heaps. Lindsey took particular delight in peeling the skin-tight breeches off of Aubrey's thighs, already slick with sweat. By the time he'd laid him bare, Aubrey had fallen back upon the bed, his prick standing taut and flush with a pearl of seed at its tip. A glance up to meet Aubrey's half-lidded eyes and glimpse of the wicked smile upon those bow-shaped lips, and Lindsey required no further suggestion to lick it clean. He savoured the taste of Aubrey upon his tongue as he circled the head of his prick, then swallowed the whole of him down. Aubrey's groan of pleasure rang in his ears. Calloused fingers ran through his hair, clenching as he traced the pulsing vein, then releasing to smooth down what they'd ruffled. A husky whisper passed over his head, too soft for him to catch its words.

Lindsey let Aubrey's prick slip from between his lips and gave him an enquiring look.

Aubrey, his pale cheeks burning scarlet with desire, spoke again, his voice louder but no less hoarse. "Come here."

Lindsey crawled up to kiss him, cradling his sharp jaw in his own soft palms.

Aubrey devoured him in return, clutching him like a man drowning—then used his hold to flip Lindsey onto his back on the bed. Lindsey offered no resistance, only moaning in protest when Aubrey pulled away.

It was then Lindsey realised Aubrey had the jar of Vaseline.

Quick as lightning, and twice as hot, Aubrey slicked his fingers and took both their cocks in his fist. They slid together in his iron grip, two swords in a single sheath, sending unspeakable sensations up through Lindsey's frame, playing his nerves like harp-strings. Lindsey's back arched beneath him, his hips rolled of their own accord, his breaths coming in desperate gasps.

Then, unaccountably, Aubrey released them.

But before Lindsey had gathered breath enough to complain, Aubrey straddled his waist, lined Lindsey's prick up with his hole, and leaned back upon it—just as he had the very night he'd claimed Lindsey for the first time.

Now, as then, the sensation of slipping inside—his sensitive cock-head squeezing through that tight ring of muscle, and the swift, slick thrust of his length following, engulfed in a passage soft as velvet and blazing hot—drove all thought from his head, and cast him into blissful oblivion, threatening to send him over the brink in an instant. He held on by his nails, digging into Aubrey's thighs with trembling hands, and feeling the flexing of powerful muscles beneath his fingertips.

Aubrey slid upwards, sacrificing almost all the length of Lindsey's prick, leaving only the head inside as he kissed him. Then back again, in one swift thrust—and forth, a kiss—and back—

At the third kiss, Lindsey loosed his hold upon Aubrey's thighs to grasp him by the shoulders and hold him in place. "For God's sake—if you don't want me to spend at once—!"

He had hardly breath enough to say it, and the kiss Aubrey used to silence him left him more breathless still. When Aubrey pulled away again, Lindsey feared himself lost, until Aubrey sat back upon Lindsey's prick and rolled his hips. A less intense yet no less enjoyable sensation for Lindsey, and, judging by how Aubrey threw his head back with a choked-off gasp, far more pleasurable for his partner.

Lindsey rolled his own hips experimentally, and knew no small measure of satisfaction as he watched Aubrey's whole frame tremble. He let his fingers fall to Aubrey's thighs again, his thumbs tracing the crest of his jutting hipbones, holding Aubrey down upon his prick as he rolled into him. Aubrey squirmed in his grasp, his own hand sliding down his front to grasp his bouncing cock. Lindsey adjusted his own grip to allow himself to join Aubrey there, to tangle their fingers together around his prick, knotting around it, twisting his wrist as he pulled. Aubrey cried out in ecstasy, leaping off of Lindsey's cock only to slam down upon it again and again, harder and harder, until—

With a final thrust down onto Lindsey, Aubrey stiffened, his back arching taut as a strung bow, and his cock pulsing in Lindsey's hand, spilling over his fingers. He trembled within as well as without, and this last sensation, combined with the sight of his exquisite pleasure, brought Lindsey to his own climax. The world faded to white, and Lindsey knew nothing beyond his own dear Aubrey.

Some moments later, he knew not how long, Lindsey roused himself to find Aubrey collapsed half on top of him, with his face nestled into his collar. Lindsey bent to kiss the crown of his head and found the scent of horses still in his hair. Aubrey stirred, lifting himself just enough to meet Lindsey's gaze with an expression as fond as his own.

"I think," Aubrey murmured, "I prefer to ride stallions."

Lindsey laughed and kissed him again.

~

CHAPTER TEN

Dear Mr Warren,

I write to humbly request the honour of your company at the — Gallery in London on the evening of Tuesday next. The painting to be exhibited, called "Icarus Fallen," will likely be of particular interest to you and your friends.

Your servant,

Mr John Halloway

Aubrey received the invitation over breakfast on Saturday. He passed it over to Lindsey, whose sapphire-blue eyes swiftly ran across the page, a handsome smile spreading on his face all the while.

"Shall we go?" he asked, returning the letter to Aubrey.

Aubrey supposed they might.

They arrived at the London house on Monday. Tuesday morning found Aubrey's stomach in knots, and this condition had not improved by evening. He donned the black tie and tails Lindsey had bought him, though his trembling fingers made the tie portion difficult. He stood in front of the washstand mirror for many frustrating minutes, until, over the shoulder of his own reflection, he caught sight of Lindsey and dropped his hands.

Lindsey, already impeccably attired and looking every inch the handsome gentleman, crossed the room with a smile. His hands alighted upon Aubrey's shoulders, and Aubrey allowed himself to be turned around to face him. Lindsey's long and elegant fingers made short work of the tie.

"I thought I might go on ahead," said Aubrey, "and meet you

there."

Lindsey paused in smoothing out the black bows and raised his brows in evident confusion. "If you'd like…?"

"It might attract attention," Aubrey explained. "For a baronet to arrive in the company of the model."

Realisation dawned upon Lindsey's features, bringing with it a crestfallen expression. Aubrey felt sorry to have prompted it, but he couldn't compromise Lindsey's reputation, and by extension, his safety. Had Aubrey a less-distinctive face, they might get away with it. But the same burn scars Halloway had rendered with such precision marked Aubrey out as the only possible model for the painting.

"I suppose it's for the best," Lindsey conceded in muted tones— yet a note of hope remained. "Halloway will look after you until I arrive."

Aubrey hadn't considered he would, though now that Lindsey mentioned it, he supposed an artist owed his model as much. "A quarter-hour's difference should suffice."

Lindsey agreed to it, and Aubrey set out for the gallery alone.

Both the London house and the gallery were in the West End, which made the walk a shorter one than Aubrey was used to. As he neared the appointed address, the number of rattling carriages and hansom cabs increased, discharging gentlemen passengers who continued on foot in the same direction as Aubrey. The reasoning for this became apparent, as the street directly outside the gallery was too crowded for through-traffic, and indeed, clusters of gentlemen in identical black tailcoats spilled out of the gallery door into the road. The murmur of the crush within rumbled outward. Before he even reached the entrance, Aubrey felt the radiating heat of the crowd. As he awaited an opportunity to slip inside, a pair of gentlemen stepped out.

"—an outrage," one gentleman said to his companion, donning his silk top hat as he spoke. "An absolute outrage."

His companion said nothing, but stroked his walrus moustache and nodded in agreement as they walked on to hail a hansom.

Aubrey's knotted stomach turned. He swallowed down his rising gall and pressed on into the gallery.

Much like the street outside, gentlemen filled the gallery interior, all speaking at once in hundreds of separate conversations rising into a mutual roar. Electric light blazed from the chandeliers to illuminate the paintings covering every inch of the walls. Waiters balancing trays of champagne flutes sailed through the crowd with well-practised ease. Aubrey found his path more difficult. The snatches of conversation he caught as he passed didn't ease his nerves.

"—absolutely disgraceful—"

"—shame to cover up such handsome features with scars—"

"Warren!"

The sound of his own name went through Aubrey's frame like a lightning bolt. He whirled around to find Halloway with champagne flute in hand and a broad grin.

"Come here," he called. "Let me shake your hand—find you a glass—no? Very well, as you wish—but do allow me to introduce you to my friend—Mr Talbot—the proprietor of this fine establishment."

Aubrey turned in the direction Halloway indicated to face an unassuming middle-aged man with both hair and moustache waxed with precision.

"How do you do," said Mr Talbot.

Aubrey replied in kind, though he couldn't help noticing how Mr Talbot's eyes had widened and his smile had frozen stiff. For, as Aubrey turned, he had revealed the other side of his face to the gallery owner, and with it, his burn scars.

"Mr Warren," said Halloway, clapping his free hand upon Aubrey's shoulder, "is the celebrated model."

Aubrey knew as well as anyone that fact was immediately obvious to all who set eyes upon both his own face and the painting, but he appreciated Halloway's introduction, nonetheless.

"Indeed," said Mr Talbot. He'd recovered most of his good manners by then, though his gaze yet lingered on the melted portion of Aubrey's ear. "I thank you, sir, for making such a splendid work possible. Your visage is a most inspiring one."

Aubrey tried not to read too much into the compliment, lest he find more insult than the gallery owner had intended, and thanked him.

"Forgive me for abandoning you so soon," Mr Talbot continued. "But I'm afraid business calls me elsewhere. Good evening, Mr Warren. It was a pleasure meeting you. I hope to see you again soon." With a bow to Halloway and Aubrey both, he vanished into the crowd as easily as a ghost.

"Talbot thinks we might have an offer on the painting this very night," Halloway announced, drawing Aubrey's attention.

"That's good," Aubrey replied, though his uncertainty turned the remark into a question.

"It's very good," Halloway confirmed. "Better than I'd hoped—though no less than I feel it deserves, if I may be honest at the risk of being arrogant. Have you seen it yet?"

When Aubrey admitted he'd not yet glimpsed the painting hanging in the gallery, Halloway bid him follow and carved a path through the crowd to the wall. Every wall in the gallery bore artworks from floor to ceiling. Yet even amongst the clutter, Aubrey's eyes immediately alighted upon the massive spread of *Icarus Fallen*.

In the makeshift studio of the Wiltshire house ballroom, the painting-in-progress had sat upon its easel at eye level with all who gazed upon it. In the gallery, it hung a little higher, forcing Aubrey to crane his neck upward towards its majesty. The painting had a glow about it, illuminating from within the pristine details of the feathers on the half-melted waxwork wings and the sculptural representation of Aubrey's own body.

"What do you think?" Halloway asked.

Aubrey didn't quite know what to think. It felt odd, to gaze upon himself from without, as a fixed image rather than the fluid and responsive reflection in a mirror. He thought Halloway had exaggerated certain features—the muscles of his arms and shoulders appeared in sharper definition than life, though still as slender as he knew his own limbs. And the burns, of course, Halloway had rendered with perfect accuracy. These, too, seemed to glow along with the rest of his flesh, as if the heat which had scarred him still blazed.

"It's... impressive," Aubrey said at last.

As he spoke, he felt his words a paltry offering in the face of the tremendous service Halloway had done to his image. Yet the wry smile on Halloway's cheek showed he understood the true meaning behind the speech, and he clapped a friendly hand upon Aubrey's shoulder before another patron demanded his attention and, with apologies, he too disappeared into the larger crowd.

Aubrey remained by the painting, alone within the throng. *Icarus Fallen* compelled his gaze for reasons apart from vanity. Yet as he looked, the conversation around him drew his attention, and he glanced about the crowd from person to person, following the snatches of speech.

"—a Romantic approach, rendered with such realism—"

"—repulsive, perhaps, but tender as well—"

"—make an offer," a silver-haired gentleman said to the gallery owner.

It took Aubrey a moment to realise the significance of this last exchange. When at last it broke over him like an Arctic wave, stopping his heart as much as his feet, he had to exert a great force of will to prevent himself from whipping his head towards the source. He resumed his lackadaisical course through the crowd until he came just near enough to observe the speakers out of the corner of his eye.

"I'm afraid," the gallery owner replied, "the work is already sold."

This revelation surprised Aubrey as much as it evidently shocked the silver-haired gentleman. A powerfully-built individual, with his black evening suit tailored to show his form off to the best effect despite or perhaps because of his age, he seemed unaccustomed to hearing he couldn't have what he wanted. Indeed, from the way his ice-blue eyes flew wide at the gallery owner's words, he found himself totally flabbergasted for the first time in all his life.

"Whatever price has been paid," the silver-haired gentleman said when he'd recovered himself, "I will double it!"

Aubrey's growing disbelief was tempered by the gallery owner's reaction. Rather than surrender to the new and no doubt astronomical bid, he simply leaned in closer to the silver-haired gentleman and, in a very low voice, hardly moving his lips, said a few short words Aubrey couldn't quite catch.

The gentleman's face drained of colour, its pallor almost matching his silver-white hair. He swallowed hard. "I see. In that case, I'm afraid I must rescind my offer."

The gallery owner gave him a gracious nod and departed, slipping back into the crowd to go about his business.

Aubrey kept an eye on the silver-haired gentleman. When the gentleman had first expressed interest in the painting, and then confirmed it, Aubrey had a moment of concern that perhaps the gentleman had been a former client of his from his days as a telegraph-boy. But upon performing the usual mental test for such a thing—attempting to picture the stranger without his clothes on—Aubrey found he had no recollection of the gentleman. He was, to all appearances, merely an admirer of art, with a passion for this work in particular.

The silver-haired gentleman watched the gallery owner's departure, then turned back to the painting. He raised his eyes to it as if compelled, and as he stood there gazing upon it, a curious expression came over his distinguished features.

Aubrey had anticipated the audience for *Icarus Fallen* would express disgust at the raw depiction of such wretched wounds. After overhearing the silver-haired gentleman's conversation with the gallery owner, he amended his prediction to account for a few individuals' lust for the nude male body on full display.

But though there was certainly desire in the silver-haired gentleman's eyes, Aubrey didn't find the lustful gleam he knew so well. Instead, the silver-haired gentleman's face showed a simple want, equal parts raw and wistful, and a slow dawning of heartbreak at the reminder that this work of art could not be his. At length, the heartbreak overcame the desire, and the gentleman turned away whilst blinking back a faint glimmer of tears.

In doing so, he turned towards Aubrey.

Aubrey quickly spun himself away from the silver-haired gentleman, but not before their gazes met. Recognition flashed in those ice-blue eyes. Rather than confront it, Aubrey dove into the crowd and let its current pull him away from his anonymous admirer.

The sea of men spat Aubrey out in a corner of the room sheltered by a fern in a jardinière. Behind the fern stood Halloway, already in conversation with the gallery owner. From the delighted look upon Halloway's face, Aubrey deduced the gallery owner had just delivered the news of the painting's sale.

"How much?" Halloway asked.

Again, the gallery owner proved the soul of discretion, leaning in to whisper the amount.

Halloway, not quite as flamboyant in expression as his other half, didn't do anything so outrageous as whoop or applaud the answer. But his eyes went very wide, and his eyebrows flew almost to his hairline, which in him was the equivalent of another man waving his hat over his head in triumph. In the next moment, his features had calmed, and he replied with a wry smile, "I wouldn't accept a penny less."

The gallery owner chuckled along in good humour. But when Halloway further enquired just who had purchased the painting, the gallery owner shook his head and murmured something which to Aubrey's ears sounded very much like, "…wishes to remain anonymous."

"If wishes were horses, beggars would ride," Halloway recited, echoing Aubrey's own thoughts.

The rest of the conversation was lost to Aubrey as just then an errant elbow from the crowd jostled him, and he turned to join the jostler in the customary exchange of "terribly sorry" and "beg your pardon."

The jostler, however, lost his voice in the midst of his "excuse me" and instead stared open-mouthed at the burnt side of Aubrey's face, which had remained turned away from him until this very moment.

Aubrey coloured and begged pardon again with perhaps less congeniality than prudence recommended. He wished he had his hat to hand, though covering his face with it would hardly make him stand out from the crowd less. The best he could manage now was slipping back into the sea of men and letting its currents toss him where they willed. Snatches of conversation flowed around him.

"—truly more akin to if Zeus had dropped Ganymede into Vesuvius—"

"—already sold! And if that shocks you, wait until you hear the price—"

"—well of course it's shocking!" came a familiar voice from the edge of the room.

Aubrey stumbled to a halt and whirled around to find the source of the outrage. There, leaning coolly against a wall with his nose in the air and a half-circle of competing Aesthetes surrounding him, was Graves.

"But sir!" one Aesthete protested. "You cannot possibly consider it beautiful—!"

"And why not?" Graves snapped. "What is beauty? That which compels one's attention, which demands response, which arrests the casual observer and forces him to confront that which will not allow him to tear his gaze away—is this not beautiful? True beauty leaves one awestruck and breathless, forever changed. One need only glance about this very room to know that *Icarus Fallen* fulfils every one of these requirements."

"You would have us believe you consider train wrecks and

industrial disasters beautiful!" scoffed another Aesthete.

"In their own way," Graves replied easily.

"Then we may toss 'ugly' out of the dictionary, for we have no further need of it, when 'beauty' may serve just as well in its stead!"

Graves curled his lip. "Certainly not, for then I would have nothing with which to describe your offensively forgettable poetry."

This sent a chortle around the half-circle, eventually even encompassing its target, though he conceded uneasily.

"But the burns, Graves!" one earnest Aesthete insisted, worrying his monocle between his fingertips.

"What of them?" Graves shrugged. "Are they not beautiful? Do they not demand attention? Do they not have the ebb and flow of a sea in a storm? Does their swirling pattern not remind one of the very foam which birthed Venus? Does their roughness not off-set and accentuate the exquisite form of the remaining flesh through contrast? I tell you they are as beautiful as the whole, and the whole would be wanting without this most vital part."

Aubrey knew such words were more likely the result of Graves's affection for the artist rather than any genuine appreciation of the model. Still, as he caught Graves's eye above the crowd, he nodded in thanks, and found the gesture returned with gravity.

Perhaps, Aubrey thought as he turned away to exit the gallery, Graves had bought the painting. For all his faults, his devotion to Halloway proved undeniable. He might very well purchase the artwork at an astronomical sum as a mere gesture of support.

However, from what Aubrey understood of Graves's finances, his share of his father's fortune amounted to little more than a fraction of what society considered truly wealthy, and while he could dole out a portion of it here or there for a fine thoroughbred or a fashionable suit, the price whispered by the gallery owner seemed a touch too rich for Graves. To say nothing of the potential gossip regarding the true nature of the relationship between patron and artist.

No, Aubrey concluded, Graves had likely not purchased the painting. If he had, he would have brought it up as a point in his argument. With a victorious flourish, no doubt.

As Aubrey moved through the crowd, he had remained so mesmerised by the question of the painting's buyer that he didn't notice Halloway in conversation with the silver-haired gentleman until he'd come within three steps of them.

Aubrey drew up short and ducked behind a convenient jardinière. While this blocked both gentlemen's view of him, he could yet overhear their exchange, and he listened intently, his heart beating a panicked staccato against his ribs all the while.

"…true masterpiece," the silver-haired gentleman was saying. "I commend you, sir, on forcing all who view it to grieve anew for the loss of Icarus. What subject shall you capture next?"

Halloway grinned. "I'm rather afraid it depends upon the whims of whoever is fool enough to commission me."

"I'm tempted to become one such fool myself," the silver-haired gentleman rejoined. "Do tell me when your next work is to be exhibited."

So saying, the silver-haired gentleman pressed a calling card into Halloway's hand and took his leave. Halloway thanked him, but the gentleman had already slipped into the crowd. Through craning his neck, Aubrey caught sight of him again just in time to watch him walk out the door and into the evening. Aubrey returned to Halloway as the latter slipped the calling card into his waistcoat pocket.

"Seems you've made quite the impression," Halloway said when he caught Aubrey's eye.

"Who was that?" Aubrey asked, making every effort to sound casual, and not as if he could hardly force the words out around his heart in his throat.

"Sir Ambrose Lockwood," Halloway answered. "Patron of the arts. Absolutely fascinated with the Classical."

"I suppose I shouldn't be quite so surprised at his wanting *Icarus Fallen* for his collection," said Aubrey.

Halloway furrowed his brow. "Does it trouble you?"

"No, no, nothing like," Aubrey hurried to assure him. "It's only…" His gaze wandered across the room towards the painting. "I've never had anyone look at me quite like that. In person or otherwise."

Halloway, too, considered the painting. "He did seem rather fond of this Icarus in particular. Though I would hope such fondness had at least something to do with my handiwork."

"Not badly, you understand," Aubrey continued, all too aware of the thoughtless *non sequitur*. "Just… different." Desire without malice, he thought but didn't say. Appreciation without a predatory element.

"I have," Halloway replied. "Seen someone else look at you like that, I mean."

Aubrey's raised eyebrows implored him to speak on.

A wry smile tugged at the corner of Halloway's mouth. "You know the gentleman in question very well. Tall, blond, affable."

Lindsey. Of course. At the mere allusion to him, Aubrey felt the knot of anxiety in his chest unravel. An unwitting smile spread across his face. He conceded Halloway's point with a nod.

Halloway looked as if he would say more, but just then another admirer caught him by the elbow, and Aubrey took the opportunity to blend into the crowd once again.

"—the model is in fact in attendance this very night! I'd thought the burns invented until I caught sight of the poor wretch—"

Aubrey forced his way between two gentlemen's backs to escape this last exchange and came out of the crowd near another painting with a far smaller audience. Indeed, most of the gentlemen peering up at it seemed only to do so in an effort to distract themselves from the wait to see the main event. But one of these gentlemen in particular caught Aubrey's attention.

Lindsey stood before the painting with his hands clasped behind his back and a contemplative expression upon his upturned face. His golden curls rose well above the roiling sea of humanity. To Aubrey, they appeared as a ray of sunshine breaking through storm-clouds.

Aubrey, not wishing to draw attention to their meeting, approached him as if he wished to gaze upon the painting rather than speak to the man. They stood side-by-side for a moment, with Aubrey watching Lindsey all the while in his peripheral vision. He thought he'd escaped even Lindsey's notice, until he detected a sparkle of joy in the corner of one sapphire-blue eye, and heard that beloved voice intone, "Good evening."

Lindsey spoke low, barely above the general murmur of the gallery, but the sound thrummed through Aubrey's heartstrings, nonetheless. He returned the greeting, still not daring to make direct eye contact until Lindsey settled the matter by turning to engage him in conversation.

"It seems to have gone over rather well," said Lindsey, smiling as one who had never doubted it would.

"You've heard, then?" asked Aubrey. When it became apparent from Lindsey's confused look that he had not, in fact, heard, Aubrey added, "It's already sold."

Lindsey appeared far less surprised by this than Aubrey felt. "Really? What a splendid triumph for Halloway. We should have him over for a congratulatory dinner."

Though Aubrey agreed with the sentiment, his own distraction prevented him from responding to the suggestion. "The buyer has chosen to remain anonymous."

Again, Lindsey seemed unmoved. "Perhaps he wishes to keep such a treasure secret from prying eyes."

Aubrey's own eyes roved over the crowd with undisguised suspicion. "Have you any idea who...?"

"Sir Lindsey!"

Both men turned to find Halloway approaching with a hand outstretched.

Lindsey clasped it with a warm smile. "I'm told congratulations are in order!"

"Indeed!" Halloway laughed. "It's enough to keep me out of the mills for another month, at least. We're going out to celebrate—Graves and some friends—once all this has died down." He gestured out across the crowd with his champagne flute. "Probably end up in Pont Street by morning. Care to join us?" His eyes turned upon Aubrey as he extended the invitation. "They'd all be delighted to meet the muse behind the work."

Aubrey looked to Lindsey for the answer, only to find Lindsey gazing down upon him with an expression suggesting it was all rather up to Aubrey to decide.

"I'm—flattered," Aubrey settled on at last. "But I'm afraid I can't tonight. Perhaps another time."

Halloway turned an enquiring look upon Lindsey, who likewise demurred.

Halloway's smile dimmed a little, but he shrugged it off. "Another time it is. We'll call it a standing invitation. Should you change your mind, you know where to find me."

Raising his glass, he slipped away into the crowd. Another cluster of admirers quickly engulfed him.

Lindsey, meanwhile, gave Aubrey a glance of equal parts curiosity and concern.

"I'm wary of parties," Aubrey admitted. Though he felt certain Halloway's party would not revolve around his own objectification, and indeed, Halloway considered him an equal in their joint creative endeavour, still he didn't think himself equal to consorting with a party of strangers. At least, not tonight. The whole of it—his past life as an object of lust in gentlemen's clubs, and his reluctance to return to anything resembling such work—remained unspoken.

And yet, though Aubrey did not speak of it aloud, still Lindsey seemed to understand it. He gave a sage nod and casually brushed Aubrey's wrist with his knuckles. Aubrey took the hint and clasped his hand. The touch lasted for but an instant, yet poured out a whole embrace's worth of comfort to Aubrey's nervous heart.

"I can get on by myself," Aubrey said, "if you wanted to go."

Lindsey shook his head, a wry smile gracing his lips. "Another time, perhaps."

Aubrey could content himself with that.

~

The exhibition lasted through the remainder of the week. Aubrey did not go to view the painting again in the gallery. Yet it did not leave his mind. Even when the exhibition closed, and the gallery shipped the painting off to its new owner, the mystery surrounding *Icarus Fallen* remained.

By then, Aubrey had returned with Lindsey to the Chorlton-cum-Hardy house. Miss Owen as housemaid and Miss Murphy as cook both flourished in their new surroundings, much to the relief of Charles. Yet the change of scene did nothing to shake Aubrey's dogged pursuit of the solution to the *Icarus Fallen* enigma.

"Who bought it?" Aubrey mused to Lindsey over dinner the evening after the exhibition's end—as he had mused many times over since the exhibition opened.

Lindsey shrugged, as he had also done many times over when faced with the very same question. "An earnest admirer of the arts?"

Aubrey carved up his *filet mignon* with a frown. "Yes, but what sort of admirer? A rich one, we must assume, but there are many sorts of wealthy people. It could be anyone from banker to baronet."

"It could…" Lindsey admitted, appearing uneasy.

Aubrey brought a bite to his lips and chewed thoughtfully. Perhaps the protein fuelled his brain, for he swallowed and added, "My hypothesis is on a more aristocratic bent. New money likes to flash it around, not buy things anonymously and hide them away where no one will see them."

"Not an American, then," Lindsey cut in with a chuckle.

Aubrey, intent on the problem, could hardly muster the ghost of a smile in response. "No, not American. And not a banker or industrialist, either—unless!" He bolted up in his seat. "Perhaps—no, impossible, and yet—could it be a woman?"

Lindsey blinked at him. "A woman?"

"A woman," Aubrey reiterated, "would have ample reason to keep her purchase a secret. You saw the crowd at the gallery."

"All men," Lindsey confirmed.

"Yes, and all in an uproar about the indignity and scandal of *Icarus Fallen*."

"I think 'uproar' is a strong word," said Lindsey.

"You cannot deny there was talk," countered Aubrey. "Some American heiress may very well have drawn upon her father's cheque-book to buy something shocking, something scandalous, to show off to her Yankee friends back home."

"There's always talk," said Lindsey, even-toned as ever.

"If the buyer has not chosen anonymity on account of their sex," Aubrey conceded, "then they must be an aristocrat. They are too proud; they do not wish to be seen throwing their money about. They wish to remain demure about their artistic tastes."

Lindsey raised one eyebrow quite high, and Aubrey belatedly recalled that Lindsey was, after all, a baronet, and therefore some manner of aristocrat, if only on a technicality.

Aubrey began stammering. "Present company—"

The rest of his apology was cut off by Lindsey's bark of laughter. Continued ripples of mirth shook his shoulders and delayed further conversation.

"For the record," Lindsey gasped when he'd recovered himself, "I have never known Graves to remain demure about his artistic tastes."

Even Aubrey had to admit that Graves, as the youngest son of a Marquess, stood a little closer to true aristocracy than a mere baronet such as Lindsey. Nor could it ever be honestly said that Graves kept quiet about his own opinions.

The appearance of Charles in the doorway of the dining room interrupted any possible counter-argument Aubrey might have formed.

"The package has arrived, sir," Charles announced. "I've brought it as far as the foyer, where I thought it best to leave it whilst you determined where in the house you wish it to make its more permanent home."

"Splendid!" said Lindsey.

Aubrey, who'd heard nothing of an expected package until this very moment, cast an enquiring look at Lindsey.

Lindsey's eyes sparkled like sunshine over ocean waves. "Would you care to come see it?"

Aubrey turned his enquiring look upon Charles, who remained as stoic as ever, before he acquiesced to Lindsey's bewildering offer and followed him out of the room.

Lindsey lead the way to the foyer. Between the front door and the staircase to the upper storey stood a shipping crate. Though taller than Lindsey, and half again as wide as it was tall, its depth measured little more than a foot. Stray tufts of straw poked out between the wooden slats.

Aubrey cast another curious glance at Lindsey. "What is it?"

Lindsey beamed down at him with the look of one with a grand surprise held close to his bosom. "Shall we peek inside?"

Charles had left a claw-hammer atop the crate, and at Aubrey's wary nod, Lindsey took it up. He pried a few slats off of one broad side with surprising capability for one not trained to labour with his hands. Tufts of straw stuffing fell out onto the floorboards—some on their own, some helped along by Lindsey's evident enthusiasm— and between the loosed slats, revealed a sight equal parts unexpected and familiar.

There, before his very eyes, stood *Icarus Fallen*.

Aubrey stared once again upon his own face in repose, rendered in oils by Halloway's paintbrush, burns and all. He continued staring for a very long moment before he turned to Lindsey.

Lindsey, meanwhile, had made some effort to bite back his smile, yet his sheer delight overpowered any attempt at restraint.

Likewise, the sight of it overpowered Aubrey's own incredulity, and he let out a bark of laughter.

Lindsey grinned freely. "Do you like it?"

"You—!" Aubrey struggled to complete his thought. Between his disbelief at Lindsey's audacity and his joy at Lindsey's satisfaction, he had another, unaccountable, even more unexpected emotion.

Relief.

No longer need he wonder who had purchased his image. No longer need he worry about whose hands his own nude form had fallen into, and to what new audiences it might be exposed. No longer need he concern himself with being put on display for untold strangers' gawking.

At his most vulnerable, Lindsey had come riding to his rescue and carried him away to safety.

Had they not, at that moment, stood in the middle of the foyer, Aubrey could've kissed Lindsey. He settled for taking him by the elbow, twining their arms together and clasping his hand very tight. Lindsey squeezed his hand in turn.

"Where shall we hang it?" Lindsey asked, jolting Aubrey out of his internal reflection.

Aubrey, having never hung a painting in his life, felt somewhat at a loss. As he considered possibilities—the morning room, the study, the library—he found they didn't feel quite right, either. None so public as the foyer, but still more public than Aubrey thought prudent. Then his mind fell upon the natural conclusion. "Perhaps the antechamber to the master bedroom?"

The moment he spoke the words, he wished he'd given them more consideration. The bedroom was, after all, Lindsey's, and not his own. It seemed a rather flagrant example of vanity to request his own visage to be displayed in a location so unavoidably intimate, to demand Lindsey confront his nude form laid out across the wall every night he spent in this house.

Still, Lindsey had asked his opinion.

And, in direct opposition to Aubrey's fears, Lindsey seemed to take no offence to the notion. On the contrary, he looked positively delighted by it.

"The bedroom, indeed!" he said, and clapped Aubrey on the shoulder.

Together, they peeled the remaining planks off of the crate, until the whole painting stood exposed. Then with Lindsey at one end of the frame and Aubrey at the other, they carried it up the stairs and down the hall to the master bedroom. A nail, a hammer, and a wire later, and *Icarus Fallen* rose into its appointed place.

"There is something haunting in it, by the gaslight," Lindsey murmured as he and Aubrey stood side-by-side in consideration of the fruits of their labours.

"Just think how it'll look under electric light," Aubrey replied.

Lindsey's face lit up at the notion. "Grand, I'd wager."

"I'd wager I could show you something grander."

Lindsey glanced down at him with a curious look. Aubrey took the opportunity to kiss him. From there, Lindsey proved quite pliable, and Aubrey guided him back into the bedroom proper, shedding layers of clothing all the way to the bed to lie side-by-side, Lindsey's lean frame curled around Aubrey's body.

Aubrey clenched his bare thighs tight, and Lindsey's cock slipped between them, sliding under Aubrey's own prick, the tip of one tracing the vein on the underside of the other with every thrust, delicious and tantalising. Then Lindsey's hand slid down Aubrey's front to grasp both their cocks. From behind his bucking hips drove Aubrey's forward in the same motion, both men thrusting as one. And all the while, Lindsey's lips fell upon Aubrey's collar and throat, pressing kisses and sucking bruises, and whispering his name into his ear. Aubrey felt Lindsey's heart thudding through his back to reverberate in his own chest, so close had he clasped him. So thoroughly claimed. So tightly embraced.

Then Lindsey's hips stuttered, and his stream of affection whispers broke off with a sudden cry as his crisis overcame him, spilling his seed into his hand and coating Aubrey's prick with it. He collapsed against Aubrey's shoulder and lay there insensible for some moments, long enough for Aubrey to turn in his arms and sidle closer to him, kissing him back to consciousness.

Aubrey's own prick still hung heavy with arousal between his thighs, and he'd almost resigned to finishing himself off, unwilling to disturb the beautiful peace of Lindsey's bliss, when Lindsey kissed him in return—first upon his lips, and then sliding lower, to his throat, his collar, and further still. Aubrey gasped to feel the fluttering touch of Lindsey's lips upon his navel. Then those same lips wrapped around his cock-head, and Lindsey swallowed him down.

Instinctively, Aubrey's fingers tangled in Lindsey's golden curls, and his hips bucked of their own accord. The ministrations of Lindsey's tongue gave exquisite pleasure, almost tormented him, until his stones drew up and his breath ceased, and he poured his essence into Lindsey, overcome by his own ecstasy.

Those long arms twined around him once again as Lindsey came up to kiss him, and Aubrey drifted off with the taste of himself on

Lindsey's tongue.

When Aubrey awoke, it was not yet dawn. The horizon had only just begun to brighten, turning the pure black of the night into an inky blue. Lindsey remained asleep, his aquiline features in repose looking not unlike an angel carved from marble. Aubrey took care not to wake him as he crept out of bed and took a candle out into the antechamber.

Icarus Fallen remained unchanged by what little time had passed—and yet, by flickering candlelight, it held a certain mystery. Aubrey gazed transfixed upon his own sleeping image for some time.

Then soft footsteps padded the floorboards behind him, and long arms wrapped around his shoulders. A familiar pair of lips pressed a kiss just behind his ear. Aubrey leaned back into the embrace.

"My very own Icarus," Lindsey whispered.

Aubrey considered the words and the painting alike. "From Ganymede to Icarus… Snatched up only to fall."

Lindsey tightened his grasp around him, a brief squeeze full of reassuring affection. "Not while I have any say in the matter."

"You'd catch me, then?" Aubrey asked, unable to keep from smiling.

"I would." Another kiss. "Besides, I think you're more of a Prometheus. Bringer of fire. Giver of light."

Aubrey wished he knew more of Classical mythology, so he might say something equally clever and complimentary in return. No matter how far he fell, Lindsey would catch him. And Aubrey could never appreciate him enough. He could damned well try, though, and to this end he turned in Lindsey's arms to kiss him. When it broke, Lindsey gazed down upon him with an expression both bemused and bashful.

"Would you have bought the painting if you didn't know me?" Aubrey asked.

Lindsey gave the painting a long and thoughtful look. At last he returned his gaze to Aubrey and spoke.

"Had I never met you—and though it pains me to consider such a world, I will do so for the sake of argument—I would still have purchased the painting. For love of the subject, of the painter's skill, and, yes, I must concede, of the model. I would have spent many hours in contemplation of the personality behind such a visage and form. I would have imagined what course our conversation might take if I should ever chance to meet him in the flesh. I would wonder if such beauty really existed in life, or if the paintbrush had conjured and shaped it." He caught Aubrey's eye with a solemn look. "I can assure you, having met the model, that while the artist's talent is great, it is not so great as to have imagined out of whole cloth the casual elegance, the raw beauty, the force which demands an otherwise casual observer must stop and stare in awestruck wonder at such a vision."

It took Aubrey a moment to recover the power of speech. "You think him rather handsome, then?"

Aubrey wanted his comment to sound playful, a lighthearted method of relieving the intensity of Lindsey's praise. The break in his voice rather spoilt the effect.

Lindsey didn't laugh at his weakness. Didn't see the break in his armour as an opportunity to press on to victory in their debate. Didn't taunt Aubrey for daring to believe himself desired still. Lindsey had never done such a thing. Lindsey never would.

Instead, Lindsey raised his hand to Aubrey's cheek, gently laid his fingers along his jawline and lifted his chin. Not forcing him to look up, and not quite giving him permission, either, but rather reminding Aubrey that he had the right to meet Lindsey's gaze. He looked deep into Aubrey's eyes, not a flicker of humour alleviating the gravity of his expression.

"Yes," Lindsey said. "I rather do."

Aubrey kissed him.

The action proved far less measured and gentle than Lindsey's words—involving both of Aubrey's hands pulling Lindsey down to meet him, fingers tangling in his golden curls, a ravenous mouth seeking to devour his. Yet it expressed much the same sentiment.

And as Lindsey melted into it, Aubrey knew he understood.

THE END

ABOUT THE AUTHOR

Sebastian Nothwell lives in Massachusetts. When he's not writing books, he is haunting libraries and museums for research to write more books. To learn more about this and other books, visit sebastiannothwell.com

16732962R00096